THOR

This edition first published in 2025 by Red Wheel,
an imprint of Red Wheel/Weiser, LLC
With offices at:

65 Parker Street,
Suite 7
Newburyport
MA 01950
www.redwheelweiser.com

ISBN: 978-1-59003-577-1
EISBN: 978-1-63341-384-9

Conceived, edited, and designed by
Quarto Publishing, an imprint of
The Quarto Group
1 Triptych Place
London SE1 9SH
www.quarto.com

QUAR: 904525

Commissioning editor: Lily De Gatacre
Editor: Charlene Fernandes
Copy-editor: Caroline West
Assistant editor: Elinor Ward
Design: Karin Skånberg
Cover and original design: Martina Calvio
Illustrator: The Saxon Storyteller
Production manager: David Hearn
Art director: Martina Calvio
Managing editor: Emma Harverson
Publisher: Lorraine Dickey

Printed in China

10 9 8 7 6 5 4 3 2 1

FSC www.fsc.org
MIX
Paper | Supporting responsible forestry
FSC® C016973

THOR

AN ILLUSTRATED GUIDE TO THE THUNDER GOD

BY L. DEAN LEE

Red Wheel

CONTENTS

CHAPTER 4: **THOR IN THE WORLD**

CHAPTER 5: **VENERATING THOR**

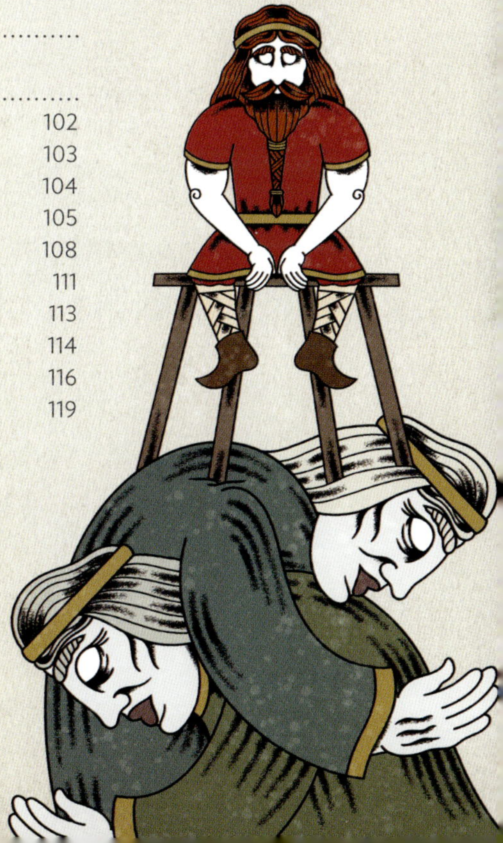

PREFACE

When I first started working with the Norse deities directly, I fell asleep one night and had a dream about Thor. He and Loki were sitting on a couch and chatting with me. I don't exactly remember what we were talking about, but I do remember one thing: Thor looked similar to the actor Chris Hemsworth, who played him in the Marvel movies of the same name.

Perhaps it's a coincidence that my first personal run-in with Thor the god reminded me of Thor the superhero... or perhaps not. After all, characterizing Thor as a superhero is not far removed from his actual function as a god: He uses his superhuman strength to fight off forces that threaten mankind, and whenever we're afraid, we can summon Thor just by calling his name.

Few archetypes are more instinctive to us than that of a hero: A hero is someone who makes people feel safe. Rescuing people, fighting bad guys, using powerful weapons, and performing feats of strength are just some of the things a hero might do to accomplish this.

But what makes the Thor of Norse mythology different from his modern-day superhero versions is the fact that his mythology characterizes him as an actual force in the world, not just a character who saves other characters within the context of a story narrative. The Norse people who grew up listening to the myths would have learned to view Thor as being as real as the storms he personifies, and that he would protect them in their time of need—a belief they took all the way into adulthood.

As early as the 1890s, the spiritual movement known as Heathenry has steadily grown in popularity. This movement is defined by a renewed interest in the old pagan practices of pre-Christian Northern Europe. The most popular form of Heathenry is currently Norse Paganism, which is characterized by veneration of the Norse gods, including Thor.

Though interest in Norse Paganism is steadily on the rise, I've noticed many people still struggle to separate the concept of "gods" from the concept of "characters." This isn't exactly a surprise; after all, many of us were taught to understand divinity through the written word, and the fact that the Norse myths move like fables doesn't help us distinguish between "god" and "character" very much.

It wouldn't be until I visited the Nordic countries that I would experience a world exactly like the one described in the Norse myths, and came to understand that the gods were first defined by this landscape, well before they were ever defined by story narratives. I looked at the peaks of Norway's mountains shrouded in mists and saw the countries of Jötunheim. I looked at the gray boulders covered in lichen and saw the trolls within. And, of course, I also looked at the thunderstorms rolling across the landscape and sea, and saw none other than the god Thor.

We don't need to go to the Nordic countries to experience the gods moving in the world around us. All we have to do is remember that this world is the context in which the gods exist. While this book is designed to introduce you to Thor, it will also teach you the skills you need to forge your own interpersonal relationship with him. The Norse gods aren't shy, least of all Thor, and he will show up if you call to him.

It is my hope that you, dear reader, will find this book an invaluable resource on your spiritual journeys.

Skål!

L. DEAN LEE

CHAPTER 1:

BRIDGING THE CULTURAL GAP

Here, we will explore the importance of the Norse gods and the purpose of mythology and folklore, and learn more about the Norse cosmos and the entities that inhabit it.

INTRODUCTION

Thor is one of the most significant gods in the Norse pantheon. Even those with only a surface-level familiarity with the Norse gods might recognize him as the thunder-god and the son of Odin.

The Norse people originated as a pre-Christian culture that lived in what we now call the Nordic countries—Norway, Sweden, Denmark, Iceland, Finland, Åland Islands, Greenland, and the Faroe Islands. Most of these countries are located in the northern European region known as Scandinavia.

The Norse people are famous for venturing out into the world as Vikings during the Viking Age (793–1066 CE) in bygone times.

However, the occupation of "Viking" was rather niche in that most of the Norse people lived out rather typical lives as farmers, craftsmen, fishermen, parents, petty highwaymen, and more.

The pagan cultures of Scandinavia began to shift with the introduction of Christianity around the start of the Viking Age. Through a process of converting Scandinavian kings, the "old ways" fell out of popularity in favor of the "new ways" of Christianity. By the end of the Viking Age, the region was fully Christian.

However, much of the Norse culture and folklore endured, and can still be found today among modern-day Scandinavians. The Norse myths and gods remain an important staple of culture in the Nordic countries today for this reason.

WHO IS THOR?

Far off in the mountains and across the wide plains, a storm cell brews. Lightning leaps from the massive clouds and strikes the Earth, and thunder booms in its wake. Rain falls, drenching the ground.

If we allow our imaginations to break free for a moment, this storm might look to us like a great lumbering figure traveling across the landscape of the world. Where is he going? What is he doing? This is something many cultures have wondered, and as a result they have decided to invent stories about it.

This particular story comes from the Norse people: This is their god, Thor, traveling on his chariot pulled by two mighty goats. He's journeying far from his home to protect humankind from the monsters known as *jötnar*, or giants, that represent the wild forces of the world and all that we fear. Thor wields a mighty, burning-hot hammer, called Mjolnir, which he uses to strike the heads of his enemies. This hammer is special in that it never misses its mark, and it will never break no matter how hard Thor throws it. The sound it makes when thrown to Earth is huge and crashing, but no matter how fearful this sound is, we can take heart in knowing it means a giant was slain, and that we now have one less thing to fear. Sometimes a rainbow appears after a storm. The Norse people had a story for this as well: This is the bridge called Bifrost (or *Bífrost* in Old Norse), which connects our material world, Midgard, to the realm of the gods, Asgard. It appears when Thor returns home after slaying giants. No giant can follow him across this bridge because the red of the rainbow is hot, which burns them up when they try to cross.

This story of Thor was told to children as a way of making the world a less terrifying place. It served the purpose of freeing their minds of both their fear of thunderstorms and their fear of the unknown; the story feels more real to the childhood imagination than the literal truth about storms.

In recent years, Thor has become a relatively well-known figure, featuring, as he does, in numerous comic books, movies, TV shows, and more. Thor's reappearance in popular culture might be because his godly role already fits so well into the superhero genre. In any case, his presence has added fuel to the fire of a growing interest in Norse Paganism.

To get to know Thor as a deity, however, it's important to understand the cultural context in which he existed; where he comes from and what function Norse mythology served. We will explore this before diving into who Thor is as a figure.

THE PURPOSE OF FOLKLORE AND MYTHOLOGY

To understand Thor, we need to understand the purpose of Norse mythology and Scandinavian folklore. Knowing what function the stories serve will lead to a better understanding of Thor's role within them.

The Norwegian writer Jan Sigurd Horn describes mythology as "[humanity's] way of expressing the knowledge we have about the metaphysical reality we believe in." We often think of mythology as a collection of static and unchanging spiritual stories, or as a history of the gods. But this impression likely comes from the fact that we often learn about mythologies through written records, which are in and of themselves static and unchanging. A living mythology is far more dynamic. Simply put, a society's mythology is the narratives it tells itself about who it is and how life works.

IS MYTHOLOGY A DIVINE HISTORY?

We might be tempted to view Norse mythology as a history of all the things the gods have done. But the Norse myths are not a history, nor can they really represent one, since they don't have a chronological order; they're only put into some kind of order when compiled in a written anthology. In addition, some stories have multiple regional variations, while others may be local to one particular community.

THE FUNCTION OF MYTHOLOGY

Mythology is a way for a culture to form an identity, an understanding of itself, and a paradigm of how it fits into the fabric of all things. It also provides a vehicle for education and a way to describe the forces and phenomena of the universe. But perhaps most of all, it's a vector through which we make sense of the world we live in and our relationship to it.

The mythology of the Norse people grew organically out of the culture itself, rather than being something that was taught to them by a religious leader or scripture. The myths are allegories that were used to explain real events, encapsulating through the medium of stories what it felt like to live on Earth.

These allegories were important because, by explaining abstract phenomena in terms of a felt-experience, the Norse people could make the world seem like a less unknowable place to live. So when they saw the edges of the world at the peaks of mountains and in the depths of volcanoes, they were already familiar with the character of these things, because of the stories they had been told of hostile giants who embodied these wild landscapes. It may have been their stories making the world a familiar place that gave the Vikings their famed courage to explore the world.

SOURCES OF NORSE MYTHOLOGY

We can often get a sense of a culture's entire mythology by looking at different records of it from different times and places, and seeing how it's changed.

Unfortunately, Norse mythology has very few things to go by. Despite the fact that the Norse people had a writing system, the mythological texts that we do have mostly date from after the conversion to Christianity.

That isn't to say they can't be trusted at all, however. We're lucky to have a few very important snapshots of Norse mythology that we can reasonably assume are authentic.

The Poetic Edda

The *Poetic Edda* is collection of anonymous Old Norse poems, many of them pertaining to the gods. There are several versions of the *Poetic Edda* in existence, many of which can be found in the *Codex Regius*, an Old Icelandic manuscript thought to have been written around 1270 CE. Even though the *Codex Regius* (which means "Royal Book" or "King's Book") was written nearly 200 years after the Christianization of Scandinavia, the stories contained within are much older, and represent the pre-Christian mythology of the Norse people.

The Prose Edda

The *Prose Edda* is a mythography written by Icelandic lawspeaker and politician Snorri Sturluson in around 1220 CE. The book is divided into three parts: *Gylfaginning* ("The Tricking of Gylfi"), *Skáldskaparmál* ("The Language of Poetry"), and *Háttatal* ("Tally of Meters"). The first two books, *Gylfaginning* and *Skáldskaparmál*, recall a series of myths and legends about the Norse gods.

Despite the fact Snorri was a Christian politician writing for a Christian audience during a time when paganism was heavily frowned upon, he actually did a great deal to preserve the Norse myths in their original form, wrapping them in a very thin disclaimer of "these aren't really gods, but nobles from Troy!" before launching into the Norse tales as they would have likely been remembered.

The purpose of the book was a political one. Snorri wanted Iceland to unite under King Hakon the Fourth of Norway, and wrote the *Prose Edda* as a way to demonstrate Iceland's and Norway's shared cultural heritage. His work remains a critical touchpoint for Norse mythology today.

Other Sagas

Many other sagas and histories, predominantly Icelandic, exist that point to different aspects of Norse mythology, folklore, and worldview, such as the *Völsunga Saga* and *Gesta Danorum*. While some of these texts mention Norse mythology and paganism, it is not always in a flattering light since they were written post Christianization.

Oral Traditions

Even to this day, remnants of the Norse myths and folklore permeate the oral traditions of Scandinavia and Iceland, circulating among society and among people who still practice Norse Paganism.

HOW DO WE DEFINE A "GOD"?

Different cultures have different ways of viewing the world, and that includes how they view deities. To know who Thor is, we need to understand how gods function within Norse cosmology.

As a polytheistic belief system, the Norse cosmology is characterized by the presence of multiple deities. Deities of all religions often have their origins in stories of once-living people and their deeds or grow out of personifications of worldly phenomena, such as death, the movement of the sun and the moon, or the activity of volcanoes. But how a culture views their deities—and the kind of relationships they have with them—varies from culture to culture.

Exactly how the Norse people viewed their own deities is tough to pin down. What can be said, however, is that they did not characterize the gods as all-powerful or as having total control over the heavens, the Earth, and fate. The Norse gods were wise and capable, but also extremely human in character, and not immune to making mistakes or being overpowered or outsmarted. They could also die, interestingly enough, though "death" was characterized as "going to a different place," rather than transcending the world or ceasing to exist entirely.

A popular impression people have of deities is that they're rulers or "lords" of certain domains. While this may be true for some pantheons, it's not quite true for the Norse one. Rather, the Norse gods tend to embody the dimensions of life in which they dwell, having been "shaped" by those things in the same way people are shaped by the landscapes they have lived in and the experiences they've had. Thor may be the god of thunder, but in this case it means that he personifies it rather than owns it in any way.

BLURRY DEFINITIONS

The lines between deity, spirit, and ancestor have a lot of overlap, since all three were venerated in Norse society. In contemporary Norse Paganism, this is much the same. A "god" is more of a function than a "type" of being, especially considering that gods can come from many different places, and the Norse gods can be referred to by many different titles.

THE TWO FAMILIES OF GODS

The Aesir

The Aesir (pronounced Ah-zir) is the principal family of deities within the Norse pantheon. They live in the settlement called Asgard, the name of which comes from the Old Norse *áss*, meaning "[a] god," and *garðr*, which means "dwelling," "farm," or "enclosure." The Aesir can be thought of as a family unit, living in their own settlement. Most of the stories about the gods focus specifically on the exploits and activities of the Aesir. Within the Norse myths, the Aesir and Asgard allegorically represent the idea of people and civilization. Thor is counted among the Aesir by virtue of the fact that he is Odin's son. Presumably, he has always lived in Asgard.

The Vanir

The Vanir is a family of deities within Norse cosmology who fought a war with the Aesir in bygone times. The Vanir are from the realm of Vanaheim, which is characterized as lush, green, and mild in weather. The gods from Vanaheim are also characterized as having these qualities, associated as they are with gentle weather and fertility.

THE NORSE COSMOS

In Norse cosmology, there is not simply one Earth or one heaven, but rather Nine Realms—multiple cosmological worlds, all connected by the branches and roots of the World Tree, Yggdrasil.

1 Asgard **2** Vanaheim **3** Alfheim **4** Midgard **5** Muspelheim **6** Niflheim **7** Jötunheim **8** Nidavellir **9** Svartalfheim

The names of the nine realms are never specifically listed, and the realms that do show up in the *Prose* and *Poetic Edda* tally up to be far more than nine. Nevertheless, a few thinkers have tried to deduce what the Nine Realms might be, if there were, indeed, a canonical nine. Henry Adams Bellows, who translated a version of the *Poetic Edda* in 1923, suggested the following potential list:

Asgard ("the farm of the gods") is the home of the Aesir. It is where many of the gods keep their halls, including Thor's hall in Asgard, Bilskirnir, which contains 540 rooms. Connecting Asgard to Midgard is the bridge Bifrost, which is represented by the phenomenon of the rainbow.

Vaneheim ("home of the Vanir") is home to the Vanir gods, such as Frey, Freyja, and Njord. Vanaheim is characterized as lush green lands with mild weather.

Alfheim ("home of the elves") The term "elves" is similar to "fae" in the sense that it's a catch-all for a variety of otherworldly beings. The elves of Alfheim are said to be the *Ljósálfar* or light elves. Alfheim was given to Frey by the gods.

Midgard ("middle Earth") is the tangible world around us—the home of mankind and all the plants and animals that live herein. Midgard is characterized as "an enclosure," a self-contained environment that is simultaneously the abode and the barrier that contains the abode and keeps the wild forces, like giants, out. In this way Midgard can be thought of a bit like a terrarium.

Muspelheim (meaning uncertain) is a primordial world like Niflheim; it's a world of heat and flame. Fire-giants, including Surt, live here. During the creation of the world, Muspelheim was pushed far above Midgard and is kept separate from it via the barrier of the sky. As the sky was being propped up, some sparks escaped Muspelheim and these were fashioned into the stars.

Niflheim ("world of mist") is a cold and misty primordial realm of frost and ice. It is where the sulfuric Elivagar rivers run from the bubbling wellspring, Hverglmir. Niflheim overlaps with Helheim and Niflhel, abodes of the dead. During the creation of Midgard, Niflheim was shoved far below the ground so it would not freeze the world.

Jötunheim ("giant country") is the home of the giants. It is mountainous, wild, and inaccessible by usual means; often the gods have to make their way across bodies of water or fly by means of magic to reach it.

Nidavellir ("dark downward country") is the home of the dwarves, master craftsmen and smiths. Nidavellir may be an abode within Svartalfheim or they may be one and the same. It is also called Myrkheim, or "dark abode."

Svartalfheim ("world of the black elves") is the home of the *Dökkálfar*, the dark elves who live beneath the earth and have a nature quite unlike that of their light-elf counterparts. The gods visited Svartalfheim to acquire Gleipnir, the fetter made of impossible things that was used to bind Fenrir.

ASGARD, THRUDHEIM, AND BILSKIRNIR

Thor lives in Asgard, the world where the Norse gods reside. The name Asgard means "farm of the gods," and according to Snorri Sturluson is said to be located "in the heavens," which can be interpreted as an astral plane or separate dimension of sorts.

When Thor visits our plane of Midgard, he often appears in the form of a storm. After the storm, rainbows appear. The Norse people had a special legend about the rainbow; it was seen as a bridge, called Bifrost, connecting Midgard to Asgard, and Thor would drive his chariot across it to return home after slaying giants. The red of the rainbow burned so hot that no giants were able to follow Thor back to Asgard; only the gods could handle the heat.

Asgard is a place of gleaming gold and silver, with a mighty stone wall and a great green field where the Aesir play games. It's also filled with many, many halls, all of which are owned by one god or another.

Now, the specific details we know of Thor's hall are a little incongruent across all historical sources, but it's said to exist

in a country called Thrudheim, meaning "world of strength." Thor's hall itself is called Bilskirnir, which means "lightning-crack." But even though it's located in Thrudheim, which is situated outside Asgard, this hall is said to exist inside Asgard. Is this just an error, or is there more to it than that?

The configuration of Thor's hall in relation to Asgard and Thrudheim might make more sense if we think of it this way: Like most things that reside "in the heavens," the "world of strength" is not describing a physical location, but rather a specific environment. When we go to the gym to lift weights, for example, we experience the "world of strength" within our bodies. We can think of this internal environment as being the country that overlaps with Thor's hall in Asgard, effectively making our workouts an act of "visiting Thor's home." It's no wonder then that so many Heathens devote exercising to Thor!

Thor's hall is also said to be the most magnificent of all the halls, with a total of 540 rooms in which gods dwell. Curiously, this also reflects the number of doors in Valhalla. It's possible this is due to a conflation between Valhalla and Bilskirnir, but it's also possible that this number was intentionally repeated for both halls. After all, 540 is a multiple of 9, and 9 is a sacred number in Norse cosmology. It wouldn't be out of the ordinary to have numbers like this intentionally repeated.

Little else was recorded about Thor's hall beyond these few descriptions. Unlike Valhalla, we don't know what it looks like or how it's decorated, nor do we know which particular gods reside within its 540 rooms.

THE NORSE ENTITIES

Norse mythology and Scandinavian folklore are filled with a number of beings. Many of these tend to be non-taxonomical in nature, and some may blend in with others. Here is a selection of the many different entities commonly mentioned in the stories.

NORNIR

The *Nornir* or the Norns are female deities who shape the course of fate and destiny. The key three are named Urd, Verdandi, and Skuld, whose names mean "became," "becoming," and "shall be." They have a well at the base of Yggdrasil from which they draw sacred water. This they pour on Yggdrasil to rejuvenate it. Other Norns were thought to exist and visit newborns to determine their future.

VALKYRJUR

Valkyrjur or valkyries are the women who ride over the battlefields and carry fallen warriors to Sessrumnir and Valhalla after they die. The word valkyrie means "chooser of the slain." Valkyries are sometimes depicted riding horses or transforming into birds, and they have their own stories in the Old Norse sagas.

EINHERJAR

Einherjar are the warriors who die in battle and are then chosen for Odin's hall. The *einherjar* feast and skirmish until Odin calls on them to fight during Ragnarok. The word *einherjar* literally means "army of one," or "those who fight alone."

ALVAR

Alvar is the term for elves, and they are depicted in many ways. There are the light elves who live in bright, heavenly planes and the dark elves who live deep in the earth—these may or may not be the same as dwarves. They are sometimes characterized as tall and sometimes small.

WIGHTS

"Wight" is a general term for "spirit," and can refer to any sort of entity in general. It comes from the Old Norse word, *vættr.*

LANDVÆTTIR

Landvættir are land spirits, beings who embody or personify a specific landscape or environment. The land itself is the spirit's corporeal form.

NISSE/TOMTE

Nisse or *tomte* are house spirits, rather like brownies or gnomes, who are thought to relate to the luck and prosperity of the home. Not all homes were thought to have a nisse, but if one moved in, it was important to make sure it was happy and included in the goings-on of domestic life. Part of that involved keeping the house tidy and leaving offerings of porridge (with butter) by the fire for them.

TROLLS

While characterized in fairy tales as creatures with cow tails that turn to stone in the sunlight, trolls as actual spirits have a much broader definition.

In the Scandinavian languages, *troll* tends to denote anything that is "other," and the word has connotations of magic and sorcery. Trolls may take on any number of appearances: boulders, cats, people, non-corporeal beings, and more. What makes something a troll has to do with the quality it possesses, rather than its physical appearance. Trolls in many ways are similar to *jötnar*.

VÖLUR

Völva (plural: *völur*) is the Old Norse word for a witch, seeress, or wise woman, and means "staff bearer." The *völur* would have practiced a kind of magic known as seid (Old Norse seiðr), which was used for prophecies, portents, and otherworldly travel. The word *spákona*, meaning literally "prophecy woman," was used interchangeably with *völva*.

JÖTNAR

Jötnar (singular: *jötun*) are beings who embody the wild, untameable landscapes and forces of the world. They dwell in places where people can potentially visit, but can't permanently live in—in extreme heat, in extreme cold, on the peaks of frozen mountains, in the hearts of volcanoes, in the depths of the ocean, in the depths of winter, and so on. Their realm is called Jötunheim.

Jötnar are referred to as "giants" in English, though they are not always large in stature. Their "giant" nature comes from the energy of their presence, which feels wild, unrefined, and big. If people are like polished jewels, then *jötnar* are like raw ores. Many of the Norse gods are *jötun* or part-*jötun*.

THURS

Thurs are giants who represent forces actively hostile toward human life—volcanic eruptions, rockslides, avalanches, and so on. The hostility of these forces is allegorically represented as "a hatred for humans" in the Norse myths. While typical giants can potentially be sociable, this is not true of the thurs.

The word "thurs" comes from the Old Norse word *hrímþursar*, which is often translated as "frost-giant." But just as *jötnar* doesn't really mean "a large humanoid," so *hrímþursar* doesn't really mean "a large humanoid frost-elemental." The implications are more along the lines of "the hostile forces that dwell at the frozen edges of the world."

Terms like "frost-giant" and "fire-giant" denote the environment the giant lives in, rather than different types of giants.

DVERGR

Dvergr or dwarves are said to live deep beneath the earth. They are characterized as masters of craftwork, particularly when it comes to smithing enchanted or impossible objects. The dwarves are responsible for creating some of the most exceptional treasures belonging to the Aesir, including Thor's hammer.

CHAPTER 2:

WHO IS THOR?

Thor is one of the most well-attested gods in the Norse myths, being the figure most often spoken of by people and seen in the world (in the form of thunderstorms). Here, we look at the origins of Thor's name, his personality, characteristics, and associations, and also learn more about those close to him, who have shaped him into the god he is today.

THOR'S NAME

The name "Thor" is the anglicized form of the Old Norse *Þórr,* and is found in a few different languages. His name is rendered as "Thunor" in Old English, "Thunar" in Old Saxon, "Thuner" in Old Frisian, and "Donar" in Old High German. These names all come from the Proto-Germanic word *Þun(a)raz*, meaning—unsurprisingly—"thunder."

Like many other Norse gods, Thor has a number of different names and kennings by which he is known in the myths. Some of the common ones include Hlorridi (which potentially means "the loud rider" or "loud weather-god"), Oku-Thor ("driving Thor"), Asa-Thor ("Aesir-Thor"), and Hardhugadr ("strong spirit").

Thor's name is also sometimes associated with the rune Thurisaz (ᚦ) since the Old Norse version of his name, *Þórr*, begins with this character. In runecasting, this rune is typically associated with the thurs (see page 21) and the strife they cause, but sometimes it's interpreted as Thor's hammer.

THOR'S PERSONALITY

The stories, myths, and cultural notions surrounding Thor paint a clear and consistent picture of who he is as a god. Some of the more prominent features of his personality are detailed here.

FRIENDLY

Thor is known for being a sociable god and for having a good and friendly temperament around people. He's not choosy about who he enjoys being around, simply relishing the company of those he's with, which is why Thor is one of the easiest of the Norse gods to get along with. He's not one for needlessly complicating relationships for any reason.

You don't always need an important reason to call upon the gods, but this is especially true for Thor. He's happy just to be asked to keep people company, and will treat this request with the same attentiveness as he does his "important godly matters" of protecting people.

SUPPORTIVE AND HELPFUL

Similarly, Thor is happy to offer us his friendship, lend his help, and support us. He can provide a listening ear when we need one and help boost our morale in particular. In some ways, Thor also embodies the spirit of people cooperating with each other and working together as a team. The Norse myths often depict Thor as a hero who single-handedly fights off the giants, but this is to impress his might upon those who are reading and listening to the stories. As a god of common people, Thor operates in a very similar way to ordinary folk, in that he embodies our cooperative spirit and our penchant for working together. Next time you are stuck on something, ask Thor for help. Even if he doesn't have a solution, he may know where to find one.

PROUD

Thor is a proud sort, but this is a positive kind of pride rather than something with a negative impact, like arrogance. It was considered good in Norse culture to feel proud of personal accomplishments and to have things to boast about.

When Graybeard the ferryman didn't recognize Thor, he immediately began to boast about who he was, knowing full well that his reputation—which he earned from his deeds—preceded him (see *Thor Argues with Graybeard the Ferryman*, pages 80–83).

Likewise, when Thor's three-year-old son, Magni, lifted Hrungnir's leg off Thor after the giant fell on him, he immediately began to boast about the greatness of his son, even giving him the fallen giant's horse, Gullfaxi, as a gift (see *Thor Fights the Giant Hrungnir*, pages 76–79).

This is the way of it with Thor. He will find things to be proud of, as well as things that are worth our pride. He will encourage us to relish in our achievements and also to accomplish things we can be proud of.

SHORT-TEMPERED

Thor is known for having a fiery temper. While he tends to be far more patient with people these days, this wasn't always the case. In fact, the Norse myths often depict him losing his patience with Loki, and the constant rage against him and threats on his life play a major role in transforming Loki from a mischievous prankster into a malicious antagonist. This isn't because Thor likes picking on Loki in particular, and Loki is not the only person he's shown to get mad at in the myths.

Thor embodies the thunderstorm, and just as Loki's mischief is part of who he is, so Thor's anger is part of who he is. But these days he knows how to use this anger productively, as opposed to simply acting upon it whenever it rises in him. Thor can get frustrated with circumstances and doesn't exercise much patience over issues that confound him, but he knows not to take this out on people, blame them for it, or frankly make it their problem in any way.

PRAGMATIC

Thor is a practical god and takes a pragmatic approach to life. After all, this is the guy who bashes giants over the head first and asks questions later. But it's not as though Thor is simple-minded—he can be clever when he needs to be. He just prefers to take a direct and straightforward path when it comes to navigating situations.

This can be refreshing at times, especially during those moments in life when things start feeling too complex, or when we're caught up in overthinking. Thor will look at a situation and call a spade a spade. In this way, he can help us get to the heart of what's important and give us practical steps for tackling life's problems.

THOR'S APPEARANCE

The appearances of the Norse gods aren't usually described in the myths, with the exception of any notable features or characteristics they may have. This is what makes Thor particularly unique, however, because we know exactly what he looks like.

HAIR AND BEARD

In the myths and oral traditions, Thor is depicted as having bright red hair and a bright red, bushy beard. Along with his wife, Sif, he's the only god whose hair has been definitively described.

However, there's another depiction of Thor at the beginning of Snorri Sturluson's *Prose Edda*, which says that he has golden hair. But this is a very euhemerized version of Thor, and in this account he's depicted as a human prince rather than a god, and not the son of Odin. (It's unclear why Snorri made this change, as he goes on to recount the Norse myths as they were otherwise originally told.)

HUGE AND STRONG

Thor is known for his might, strength, and enormous size. These attributes may have been inspired by the storm clouds he also represents. There are legends in the myths and in Scandinavian folklore that describe Thor carving out the valleys between mountains with his hammer, which shows just how large he can be.

Thor's large size seems to change depending on the context, though. He is generally depicted as being proportional to his fellow Aesir, and in some cases confronts giants far bigger than he is.

FLAMING EYES

Thor is said to have a quick temper. Whenever he gets angry, his eyes burn with bright flames. Everyone from giants to gods find Thor's burning eyes to be shocking and even intimidating, because it means that he is only a few moments away from picking up his hammer and bashing them with it.

THOR'S CHARACTERISTICS

Now that we have an understanding of Thor's personality and appearance, we can move on to his characteristics, as they define who he is and what his nature is, all of which are important for our perception of him.

PROTECTOR OF MIDGARD

This is not only a catchy phrase used in Marvel's *Thor* movies for the superhero, but a title held by the actual god Thor in Norse mythology as well. His primary role as a deity is to protect humankind, which is demonstrated by him fighting off malicious giants that would otherwise harm human beings.

Thor was perhaps the Norse people's solution to two major fears that we experience when young: Things that go bump in the night and thunderstorms. By personifying thunderstorms as a protector-spirit that keeps the nighttime monsters at bay, children would no longer fear the natural forces of the world. Instead, they would sleep well, knowing that Thor—the thunderstorm—would never let the dark things that twist in the fog of mountains reach them.

Thor's protection wasn't only for children, as they carried the certainty of his protection into adulthood, where it served more or less the same function as it did when they were young. Knowing Thor was there watching over them made them feel safe and secure in the world, and gave them the courage to explore it.

MIGHTY

Though many Aesir are warriors, Thor is considered the strongest and mightiest of them all. Very few giants are willing to contend with Thor, despite being ready to take on the entire host of Aesir.

In some areas of the world, Thor's might is also revealed in legends of him flattening mountains into valleys

NOTABLE POSSESSIONS

Many people know of Thor's mighty hammer, Mjolnir, but he actually possesses two other crucial items that are blessed with magic.

MJOLNIR

Thor has a powerful weapon that he uses to fight off *jötnar*: a hammer called Mjolnir. Written as *Mjölnir* in Old Norse, the name simply means "crusher."

Mjolnir was forged out of iron by the crafty and clever dwarves, who can make anything they put their minds to (see *The Cutting of Sif's Hair and the Forging of Mjolnir*, pages 48–53). But thanks to Loki's meddling, Mjolnir sustained a characteristic flaw—its handle is short compared to its head. It is nevertheless perfect for Thor and otherwise retains all its incredible properties: It always returns to the hand that throws it, never misses its target, and burns bright-hot. What's more, Thor can throw his hammer as hard as he wants and it will never break.

Mjolnir is an allegory for lightning. The sight of lightning striking the sides of mountains may have inspired the image of Thor throwing his hammer against the heads of giants.

Mjolnir has also been used as a tool for resurrection in the Norse myths. Thor can slaughter his goats, eat them, and resurrect them good as new, so long as the bones are left unharmed and thrown back on the goatskins. He resurrects his goats by waving his hammer over the skins and bones (see *Thor and Loki Visit Utgard-Loki*, pages 62–69).

BELT OF STRENGTH

Thor also owns a belt of strength called *Megingjörð*, which translates as "power-belt." True to its name, this belt amplifies Thor's already formidable strength. The word *megin* has a nuanced meaning within Norse metaphysics. *Megin* is a power derived from having a greater connection to the ecosystem of all things. If we are divorced from a strong community, the environment we live in, the spirits around us, or even ourselves, we become depleted of *megin*, personal strength, by virtue of the fact we are less connected to the things around us and therefore have less connection to the power of all things.

Thor's belt of strength allows him to draw from the power of all that he's connected to in order to amplify his physical might.

IRON MITTS

Thor possesses a pair of iron mitts called *Járngreipr* (or "iron-grippers"), which he wears to handle the burning-hot Mjolnir. There is very little mention of these iron mitts in the Norse myths, so they could just as easily be used to protect Thor's hands from the impact of Mjolnir flying back to his hands.

THOR'S ASSOCIATIONS

Thor has many defining qualities and associations, given his connections to people, worldly phenomena, and the general goings-on of life. For a god who lives in the realm of Asgard, he is very involved in Midgard, looking out for us and caring for our wellbeing.

STRENGTH

As a protector deity, Thor is associated with strength, particularly with feats of power and great physical might. Even Thor's hall in Asgard, called Bilskirnir, means "strength." The halls in Norse myths are metaphors for the different faculties and experiences we have as humans, which suggests Thor "lives" in any circumstance that engages our strength.

We don't need great physical strength to venerate Thor, but it's common for Heathens to dedicate different feats of strength to him as a form of worship, or even just to show appreciation. We can likewise call on Thor to help us find strength when this is needed in our lives.

COURAGE

In addition to strength, Thor is closely associated with courage. The word "courage" comes from the French word *coeur*, meaning "heart," so this is more than just a show of bravery—courage is the circumstance of having passion and caring very deeply, to the point it can drive us to overcome the state of fear.

Thor can also teach us something about where true courage comes from—not from the desire to escape feelings of fear, but from accepting fear as a natural part of being courageous. It's only by accepting the existence of fear, rather than conquering it, that we can develop Thor's great level of courage.

Thor's immense courage arises from the fact that he knows exactly what he's capable of and where that great capability ends. When he reaches the point of uncertainty, he knows when to turn to others for help.

We can call upon Thor to help us find the courage in life to face our difficulties, from everyday fears to truly unique circumstances. We don't have to worry about any fear being too ridiculous for Thor, because he will support us through everything, no matter what.

PROTECTION

Naturally, Thor is associated with protection, being the Protector of Midgard and the people within it. The Norse believed that all they had to do was call Thor's name, and he would be there by their side. This still holds true to this day and has not changed for the hundreds of years Thor has been around.

The Norse also made pendants that looked like miniature versions of Thor's hammer, which gave them a sense of courage and safety in the world. These hammer pendants still exist today. Some are replicas of ancient designs, while others are completely new. Their meaning hasn't changed much either; wearing a Mjolnir pendant bestows Thor's protection upon the wearer and keeps them safe. Pendants can also be gifted to others to bestow protection on them.

THE COMMON PERSON

Thor is the patron deity of common people: farmers, smiths, laborers, and any and all "blue-collar" workers. This is not to say that he doesn't care about white-collar workers, of course, but it means he'll always stick up for the little guy and stand for the common person. There's a potential historical reason for this; Thor was the god of commoners rather than outliers like poets, kings, and so on. This is very much in contrast with other Norse gods, such as Thor's father Odin, who was viewed as the patron god of kings, warriors, and the wealthy; Bragi, who was the patron of poets; or Njord, who was the patron of sailors.

Today, the Norse gods interact with all people regardless of their wealth, status, class, or occupation. However, Thor's skills and specialty remain squarely with the goings-on of the average person, rather than in anything specialized such as sailing, poetry, or diplomacy. It's no wonder, then, that so much of Norse mythology features Thor as a primary character—he was worshipped by the most people!

STORMS

Thor is associated with thunderstorms and lightning. If you've ever seen a storm cell moving over fields or mountains, you've seen Thor driving his goat-drawn chariot over Midgard.

That's right. Thor isn't the creator of storms. He *is* the storm.

Our logical mind may not like this idea very much. After all, we know the scientific reason behind storms: that they're the product of moisture and hot air interacting with cold air. We also don't typically think of weather patterns as "beings" in any way.

But this "rational" view of storms goes out the window the moment we're caught in one; faced with thrashing rain and lightning, we'll beg the storm to please let up, to move in a different direction, or to avoid striking near us.

It's not as if we're suddenly under the impression that the thunderstorm is a living organism like us, nor are we suddenly plagued by superstition that it might be out to get us. When faced with the imminency of something like a storm, we default to a much older instinct of interacting with phenomena: in the same way that we interact socially with each other. (Scolding inanimate objects for not cooperating is also part of this instinct.)

Like us, the Norse people knew storms were the product of weather patterns; they would have needed to know this in order to sail ships and grow crops. But if they were just as knowledgable as us about the weather, why would they still portray storms as a god? It's because our understanding of the world becomes richer, deeper, and more complete when

we also include the way our mammalian brain understands it. The Norse didn't favor the "rational" mind at the expense of the mammalian one, and instead utilized both.

Portraying storms as a protector-deity was also useful. Not only did it teach children to view thunderstorms as something good rather than a force to fear, it likewise encouraged them to think about the world within a social frame of mind. Encouraging this social mindset helped them grow into sociable people, which counteracted problems such as delinquent behavior and misanthropy, and by extension prevented needless fighting, murder, and the like.

So, next time you see a thunderstorm, allow yourself to say: "That's Thor," and see how that feels deep within.

FERTILITY

Interestingly, Thor's hammer is also portrayed as a device for consecration and fertility. When Mjolnir is stolen by the giant Thrym, Thor disguises himself as Freya—Thrym's would-be bride—to get it back. During the wedding ceremony, the hammer is set on Thor's lap in order to "consecrate the bride" (see *The Theft of Thor's Hammer*, pages 54–57).

This might have something to do with the fact that Thor's wife is Sif, the goddess of wheat fields. Picture for a moment the image of a storm rolling over a golden field of wheat. Rather than destroying the wheat, the storm instead nourishes it and makes the land fertile. The Norse people may have placed a hammer on the lap of a new bride as a way to bless her with healthy children.

THOR'S FAMILY AND IMPORTANT RELATIONS

Thor is not just a solo figure, but someone with a large family. A few of his most significant family members are featured below and on the following pages.

From left: (behind) Tanngrisnir, Balder, Bor, Bestla, Nott, Loki; (front) Jord, Frigg, Odin, Thor

From left: (behind) Sif, Jarnsaxa, Modi, Magni, Thrud, Ullr; (front) Thjalfi, Roskva, Tanngnjost

THOR'S FAMILY TREE

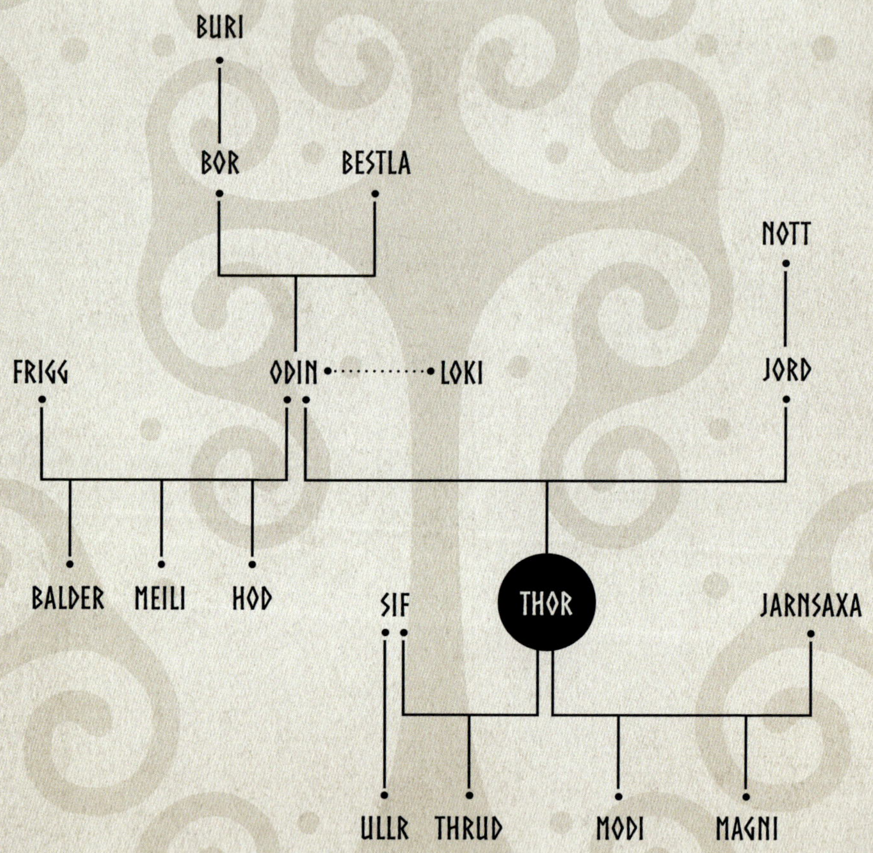

ODIN

Thor's father is the god Odin, the Allfather, and his mother is the giantess Jord. Not much is known about Thor's conception, but since Odin represents war and intellect, and Jord the solid material world, then it's easy to see how these two coming together would create Thor, the thunderstorm—something that is both a natural phenomenon and of a war-like nature.

Odin is sometimes known to test Thor's mind, not sparing him simply because he is his son. While Thor received his warrior prowess from his father and his giant-strength from both his parents, he tends not to spend time in the same intellectual realm as his father, preferring "street-smarts" over Odin's complicated riddles.

JORD

Thor's mother is a giantess named Jord, who personifies the Earth. She doesn't appear much in Norse mythology, but when she does, it's always in the capacity of Thor's mother. We can assume that Jord was one of Odin's consorts, as she was never married to him. Despite being a giantess, Jord is sometimes regarded as an Aesir, and she has certainly never demonstrated the hostile nature characteristic of unfriendly giants who dislike society.

NOTT

Nott is Thor's maternal grandmother, and she personifies the night. She is dark, as was typical of her family, and had Jord with a man named Annar.

BOR

Bor is Thor's paternal grandfather, who had Odin with his wife Bestla. Bor was the son of Buri, who was licked out of primordial ice by the cow Authumbla.

BESTLA

Bestla is Thor's paternal grandmother, a giantess. We know little about her, but she was presumably far more beautiful and less wild than the other *jötnar*, which is why Bor took her as his wife.

FRIGG

Frigg is Odin's wife and Thor's stepmother. She is associated with weaving and women's mysteries, and said to be as wise as, if not wiser than, Odin himself. We don't see her interacting with her stepson very much in the Norse myths, but we can assume they get along.

JARNSAXA

Jarnsaxa is Thor's consort and she is a giantess whose name means "iron dagger." She is also one of the nine mothers of the god Heimdall, who is the watchman of the Aesir. Jarnsaxa and Thor had a son together, Magni, and she's potentially also the mother of Thor's other son, Modi.

SIF

Sif is Thor's wife and a goddess associated with wheat fields. And just as these have long, beautiful, golden grasses, so Sif has long, beautiful, golden hair. Thor loves his wife very much, and when Loki cuts off Sif's hair as a prank, he flew into a rage and threatened Loki with physical violence unless he fixed it. Loki did this by asking the dwarves to forge a new head of hair for Sif. It's also from this escapade that the hammer Mjolnir was forged.

MODI

Modi is Thor's son, likely with the giantess Jarnsaxa. His name means "wrath." He is mentioned alongside Magni as a survivor of Ragnarok and the inheritors of Thor's hammer, Mjolnir.

MAGNI

Magni is Thor's son with Jarnsaxa and his name means "mighty." Magni plays a part in the story of Thor's battle with the giant Hrungnir, where he helps lift the fallen giant off Thor despite being only three-years old. Thor is very proud of his son for this. It is understood that Magni survived Ragnarok with his brother Modi.

LOKI

Loki is Odin's mischievous blood-brother, which makes him Thor's uncle. Loki accompanies Thor on many of his adventures. He can be a nuisance at times but also a great benefit. After all, it's thanks to Loki that Thor's hammer was created!

THRUD

Thrud is Thor's daughter with Sif. Her name means "power." She could be the same Thrud named as one of the valkyries and who serves ale to the einherjar in Valhalla (see page 20). In one story, a dwarf called Alvis claims to be engaged to Thor's daughter, who might be Thrud, and Thor, disapproving of this engagement, tricks the dwarf into bantering with him all night until he turns to stone due to the light of the rising sun (see *Thor Outwits a Dwarf*, pages 74–75).

ULLR

Ullr is Thor's stepson, a winter-god associated with skiing, hunting, and archery. Though his mother is Sif, his father is unrecorded.

THJALFI AND ROSKVA

Thjalfi and Roskva are two siblings, a boy and a girl, who act as servants to Thor. They were originally from a poor family and were given to Thor in compensation for damaging Thor's goats. Thor had slaughtered the goats for their father, a farmer, and his family to eat, saying they could be resurrected as long as the bones were left unharmed. But Loki encouraged Thjalfi to break open one of the leg bones to get at the marrow inside, resulting in that goat having a lame leg upon resurrection. So, the farmer gave his children to Thor in repayment, and they have been his servants ever since.

TANNGRISNIR AND TANNGNJOST

Thor has two goats, named Tanngrisnir (which roughly means "teeth-grinder") and Tanngnjost ("thin-teeth," with the connotation of meaning "gap-toothed"). The goats pull Thor's chariot across the sky. Why goats, you might ask? I like to think that this has something to do with the way clouds look; if we imagine puffy, white clouds to be sheep, then naturally the troublemaking gray thunderclouds would likely be goats.

HALF-SIBLINGS

Thor has many half-brothers through Odin and Frigg. This includes Balder, the shining god (illustrated above) and Hod, the blind god.

CHAPTER 3:

THOR IN MYTHOLOGY AND FOLKLORE

Let's now visit the stories of Thor as he battles giants, gains his hammer, and faces near-impossible feats of strength.

A NOTE FOR THE READER

Often when we read, we read quietly to ourselves. But to gain a full experience of the Norse myths, we must experience them the same way the Norse people did hundreds of years ago...

In 1993, the German researcher Edward Wachtel published a paper recounting an astounding experience he had while interacting with prehistoric cave art in France. The first destination on Wachtel's journey was a cave system called Les Combarelles, in the Dordogne, which was well funded and brightly lit. But Wachtel had trouble understanding the cave art he was looking at because the pictures were drawn in a way that didn't make any sense: The animals were depicted in multiple poses, with each pose etched on top of another. This mystified Wachtel until he visited his next destination in the Dordgone, a cave called La Mouthe, which was poorly marked, poorly preserved, and lacked any sort of lighting. His tour guide was a local farmer, Monsieur Lapeyre, who, instead of a flashlight, used a gas-lit lantern to guide him in the cave.

It was under these dimly lit conditions that Edward Wachtel understood why the cave paintings looked the way they did—they were meant to be viewed by the flickering light of a fire. He encouraged Lapeyre to swing the lantern while standing a few feet away from the wall, and as the farmer did so, the animals on the cave walls began to move, their pigments growing brighter or darker and their poses shifting from one pose to the next depending on where the light and shadows fell. What Wachtel didn't understand when viewing the cave art in bright light, he understood by experiencing it in the conditions in which it was created; in the light of flickering fire. Wachtel saw another dimension of depth in the art that would have otherwise been absent.

Norse mythology works in a remarkably similar way, and faces a strikingly similar problem: For those of us removed from the Scandinavian oral tradition, our typical approach to the Norse myths is to read them silently to ourselves at any impersonal hour of the day. But this creates a similar effect to looking at cave paintings under bright lights—the change of medium causes us to lose an entire dimension of understanding.

In order to experience the full impact of the Norse myths, we need to replicate the conditions in which these stories were created. Fortunately, the way to do this is rather straightforward.

During the evening or at night, find time to settle down in front of a fire or some candles, or at least in an environment with a low-level light source, preferably incandescent in nature. Turn off any TVs or radios, and reduce any other considerable sources of noise. The goal is to tailor your environment to promote the sensation of "feeling cozy and content while sitting around the fire with loved ones"—a sensation known as *hygge* in modern-day Danish. The feeling of *hygge* is something that is shaped inside you by the visceral sensation of your environment. It's best not to try to "manifest" the feeling inside you based on the theoretical idea of it.

Once you've created this environment and are settled within it, the next step is to read the myths in this chapter out loud, slowly and quietly to yourself, the inner child. By "inner child," I don't mean your recollection of who you were as a child, but rather the child-mind that we all have inside us right now. This is that child's opportunity to once again experience the excitement and joy of being told a story.

It's alright if you can't do these things at this exact moment. The point of this passage is to give you the knowledge you need to experience the Norse myths when an opportunity does present itself.

It's also alright if you don't feel a sense of *hygge* right away, despite promoting it in your environment. This can happen if we lead particularly busy or stressful lives, and all it means is that our bodies need time to remember how to relax. We can encourage this by letting ourselves have the small creature comforts that bring us gladness and inner peace.

When you can, though, I encourage you to read the following myths out loud to yourself.

ROUND THE CAMPFIRE

Telling these myths around an outdoor campfire also works exceptionally well for this exercise. If you're in company, you or another member of the group may say these stories out loud. Remember to speak slowly and softly.

THE CUTTING OF SIF'S HAIR AND THE FORGING OF MJOLNIR

If Thor personifies the storm clouds, then his hammer, Mjolnir, is the lightning. Lightning striking the Earth and the sound of thunder contributed to the legend of Thor throwing his hammer. The story of the forging of Mjolnir tells how his hammer was made.

The mighty thunderer Thor had a beautiful wife named Sif, who was known throughout all the worlds for her kindness and generosity. But perhaps her most remarkable feature was her long, golden hair, which trailed at her heels and glimmered like the fine color of golden wheat.

Thor adored his wife immensely and enjoyed waking up next to her each day. He would fondly gaze at his sleeping wife, watching the sunshine light up her beautiful golden air as it spilled over the side of the bed.

But one morning Thor rolled over to look at his wife, only to see a perfectly smooth, bald head. "Sif?" he questioned.

Sif rose and looked at her husband in confusion. "Thor?" she replied. She felt her head and in the next moment screamed, all sleepiness leaving her eyes.

Thor stormed out of bed and barreled furiously down the hall. He recognized the nimble handiwork of his uncle Loki when he saw it. "Loki!" he cried angrily. "Loki, where are you?"

No sooner did Loki appear before him than Thor grabbed him by the scruff of the neck and pulled him close. "Did you cut my wife's hair?" he bellowed furiously into his face.

"Maybe," said Loki with a sly grin.

Thor clenched his fist and raised it. "If you don't go to the dwarves and get them to forge her a new head of hair this very instant, I swear I will break every last bone in your body!" he shouted.

Loki wriggled in Thor's grasp, fearing for his life. "Alright! Alright!" he pleaded. "Let me go! I'll fix it! I'll fix it!"

Thor released him and off Loki dashed, leaving Thor in the hall, fuming with rage.

Loki ran as fast as he could out of Asgard and deep down into the earth, heading to the dark, cavernous halls that made up the home of the dwarves. He knew of a very skilled set of dwarves called the Sons of Ivaldi, who were renowned for their fine work.

Loki entered their workshop and proclaimed, "The goddess Sif needs a new head of hair! One that is made of pure gold and that will take root in her head the moment she puts it on!"

Loki paused and thought, his heart still racing from Thor's threats. He said, "And while you're at it, make me a spear that never misses and a ship that can fly over land and sea! Then the Aesir will forgive me for sure."

The dwarves grumbled at these requests because they loathed doing

favors for nothing in return, but they disliked Loki causing problems for them even more. So, with a sigh, they got down to work.

First, the dwarves took some gold and threw it into the forge fires, tempering it and spinning it until it became a luxurious head of gleaming golden hair for Sif.

Then, they completed Loki's other requests, crafting a magic spear that never misses, named Gungnir, and a flying ship that would always find good winds and could be folded up like a napkin to fit inside one's pockets. It was called Skidbladnir.

"You Sons of Ivaldi are truly the best!" Loki said, looking at these treasures. "I bet there isn't anyone better at creating such fabulous things as you!"

Loki's praise was overheard by a passing dwarf named Brokk, who saw all the fine treasures and grew irritated. He walked up to Loki with a scowl and said to him, "I bet my brother Sindri is better. He could easily make three things finer than these!"

"Oh yeah?" Loki replied. "How much do you want to bet?"

"I'll bet my head on it!" Brokk said. "That is how confident I am. And what about you, Loki? Can you say the same?"

"Well of course I can," said Loki snidely. "I'll bet my head that you can't!"

"Then it's a deal," said Brokk. "I'll meet you in Asgard with three of the finest treasures you have ever seen!"

Quickly, the dwarf went home to his brother Sindri and told him about the deal, suddenly worried that he had made a grave mistake.

"You won't lose your head, Brokk," Sindri told him. "But the Sons of Ivaldi are very skilled, and if we want to outwit them, we must give it our all. Help me work the bellows of the forge! We'll have our three treasures, but only if the heat of the forge is just right. Don't let your grip slip—not even once!"

So the two dwarves got to work. Sindri put a pigskin into the forge and Brokk worked the bellows smoothly.

Little did the dwarves know that Loki had followed Brokk home. With a snigger, Odin's blood-brother took on the form of a horsefly and flew into the workshop, buzzing around Brokk's head a few times before landing on his arm and biting it. The dwarf grimaced but kept his rhythm.

Eventually, Sindri removed the first product from the fire. It was a magnificent golden boar, whose bristles shone so brightly that they were like light

streaming through the clouds. So swift was this boar that he was able to run across sea and sky faster than any horse. His name was Gullinbursti.

"That's the first one," said Sindri. "Good job keeping the fires even, Brokk."

Next he put a lump of gold into the fire and Brokk began to work the bellows as before. But Loki the horsefly buzzed around him yet again before landing on his neck and biting twice as hard. Brokk hissed from the pain but kept the fires of the forge blazing evenly.

Soon Sindri took an exquisite golden arm-ring from the flames. This arm-ring was enchanted, so that on every ninth night it would drip eight rings that looked just like itself.

"And now for the very last one," said Sindri. "And it will perhaps be my finest work yet. Brokk, you must keep the fires perfectly hot, alright? One little pause in stoking the flames could ruin everything!"

"I will," Brokk promised, and Sindri put a lump of fine iron into the forge.

Brokk worked the bellows in perfect time, but then the horsefly returned, this time landing right in the center of his forehead and biting as hard as it could.

"Ow!" cried Brokk. His hand let go of the bellows for just a moment to wipe the blood out of his eyes.

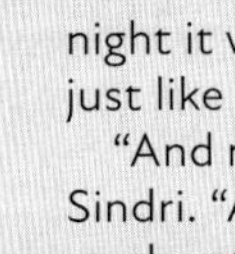

"Oh!" Sindri cried. Brokk watched his brother pull a burning-hot hammer that hummed and buzzed with lightning from the forge.

"The head is perfect, the finest I've ever made," Sindri remarked. "But the handle... well, it will need to find the right hand for it." He turned the hammer to show Brokk the handle. It was a bit short.

"But otherwise it's a fine weapon," Sindri continued. "It can break through mountains and trees and incinerate any foe. It burns white-hot and will always return to the hand that throws it. And what's more, it can shrink down to a small size and be worn around the neck! Its name is Mjolnir."

Brokk nodded, mopping the blood off his head. "Let's take what we have made to Asgard," he said.

So Brokk and Sindri took their three treasures to the home of the gods, while Loki returned with the treasures made by Ivaldi's sons.

Thor was standing at the gates with his wife Sif, who looked miserable without her head of hair. Thor himself still looked very angry.

"Well?" he asked Loki as he and the dwarves approached. Loki produced the dazzling wig of hair and handed it to Thor, who immediately placed it on Sif's head.

Thor's face lit up when he saw the hairs take root and grow, and soon his wife's head was richer and more golden than it had ever been before. Sif let out a great sigh, her mood immediately lifting.

"And now for our wager," Brokk said to Loki. "Let's have the gods decide who made the finer goods!"

So Thor, Sif, Loki, and the dwarves all gathered together in Asgard's largest field with the rest of the gods, and Loki presented the goods made by the Sons of Ivaldi.

"Here we have Sif's golden hair," he said proudly. "Finer than it's ever been before." The Aesir agreed this was true.

Loki then presented the spear, Gungnir. "This, I believe, should go to Odin," he said. "A spear that never misses."

The Allfather took it with great approval, knowing he would use it in all future battles.

Lastly, Loki took out the magical folding boat and unfolded it before their very eyes. Its great white sails billowed as it moved gracefully across the sky.

"And this, I think, should go to Frey," said Loki. "A fine ship for a fine warrior."

Frey was delighted by the boat and has used it to travel across the sky ever since.

Then Brokk and Sindri stepped forward. "Here we have the gifts made by my talented brother Sindri, whose work is the greatest there is," said Brokk.

Firstly, Brokk presented the arm-ring, Draupnir, to Odin, who was more than delighted by the implications of such endless wealth.

Then he presented the golden boar to Frey. It was such a noble animal that it took a liking to Frey immediately.

"I believe our last gift should go to you, Thor," Sindri said, approaching the thunderer. "My eyes have measured each hand of the Aesir, and I think there is no one better suited to Mjolnir."

Sindri showed the hammer to Thor, whose eyes grew wide upon seeing it. "You can strike with it as hard as you like and it will never break, and it will never miss. It will always return to your hand when you throw it," explained Sindri.

Thor took the hammer in his hand and, true to Sindri's words, it was a perfect fit for him. His gaze searched the landscape, and in the next moment he threw it as hard as he could at a nearby mountain. Boom! The hammer struck the top of the mountain, blowing off its peak, before flying back into Thor's hand.

Thor beamed with delight at this. "I love it!" he cried.

The Aesir cheered and immediately pronounced Brokk and Sindri the winners of the bet.

Brokk grinned and pulled out his dagger to remove Loki's head, but when he looked around he couldn't find him anywhere. "Where did he go?" he demanded.

Thor saw Loki sneaking out of the gates of Asgard. "Oh no, you don't!" he said. He lunged after Loki and dragged him back. "You made a wager!"

"Fine, I did!" said Loki craftily. "Brokk can have my head, that's fine... but he can't have my neck!"

Brokk grew puzzled about this and tried to work out a way to remove Loki's whole head without touching his neck. Soon he became fed up with thinking and instead pulled out a thread and an awl and stitched Loki's mouth shut.

Loki ripped the stitches out, but his face remained very sore for a long time afterward.

As for Thor, he went on to use his hammer Mjolnir to fight off the many giants that wanted to attack Asgard and Midgard. Whenever lightning strikes a mountain, that is Thor protecting mankind from the frost-giants.

THE THEFT OF THOR'S HAMMER

Thor is considered one of the manliest of the gods. However, when his hammer Mjolnir is stolen by the giant Thrym, he must go through unconventional means to get it back. Thrym will only return the hammer in exchange for Freyja as his wife... and while the Aesir do send him a bride, it isn't Freyja.

One bright morning in Asgard, Thor awoke to the sun shining on his face and a yawn escaping through the bristles of his fiery red beard. He stretched his arm out to grasp the handle of his hammer Mjolnir and lift it from its place on the side table... only for his hand to grasp empty air.

Thor's sleepy eyes snapped open and he stared at the side table in utter disbelief, looking hard at the vacant space normally occupied by Mjolnir. He scrambled from the bed and stooped over to check under the table, then under the bed, before proceeding to upend every piece of furniture in the room. But everywhere Thor looked, no hammer could be found.

Thor's patience rapidly dwindling, he grumbled before cupping his hands to his lips and shouting loudly: "Loki! Loki! Where are you?"

A few moments later, the wry-faced Loki was standing at the door, his eyes taking in the mess.

"Yes, Thor?" he asked. "Do you need help redecorating?"

The heat rushed to Thor's head at Loki's cheeky quip. "I have a bigger problem at hand," he said.

Thor leaned in close to Loki's ear, so close that his whiskers brushed against it, and he whispered, "My hammer has been stolen from me."

All the color drained from Loki's face as he heard this, his mind filling with images of angry giants besieging Asgard. He knew they would waste no time storming the gates if they heard that Thor's hammer had gone missing.

"Are you sure you didn't just leave it in the cellar?" Loki asked. Thor shook his head. "Then that is a problem indeed."

"What should we do?" whispered Thor, his face full of worry.

Loki scratched his chin and squinted. "Let's ask Freyja," he said.

So the two of them ambled over to Freyja's halls, whistling nonchalantly as they did so. But once they were in front of her, the worry returned to their faces once more.

"Freyja," Thor said. "My hammer has been stolen."

Freyja's expression turned stricken at this and her hand flew to her mouth. "... Hang on, are you sure you didn't just leave it in the cellar?" she asked. Both Loki and Thor shook their heads.

"But I was thinking... " said Loki, "... of borrowing your feathered cloak to go and search for it. Will you lend it to us?"

"I would lend it to you if it were made of silver," said Freyja. "And I would lend it to you if it were made of gold."

Freyja undid the clasp of the feathered cloak she wore and shrugged it from her shoulders, passing it to Loki.

Loki grinned gleefully as he put on the cloak, transforming into the shape of a falcon. With a few beats of his wings, he took off, flying out the doors of Freyja's hall and into the open sky.

Thor stayed behind, pacing the hall and gnashing his teeth, sometimes sitting and sometimes standing.

Eventually, Loki returned, smelling of the cold winds of Jötunheim.

"Any luck?" Thor demanded. "Tell me while you're still in the air! Tales escape a man who sits and turn to lies when he lies down!"

Loki whirled around in the air as he recalled what he had learned: "My journey took me deep into Jötunheim," he said. "There I found Thrym, the king of the giants, attending to his estate, sitting on top of a burial mound, plating his dogs' collars with gold, and trimming the manes of his horses."

Loki continued, "I asked him if he'd seen your hammer and he confessed to having stolen it and hiding it eight leagues beneath the sea. He said he will only give it back if Freyja marries him in eight days' time!"

"Eight leagues!" cried Thor.

"Eight days!" cried Freyja.

Their indignant hollering could be heard across Asgard.

Soon, word got out that Thor's hammer had been stolen, and Odin quickly called for an assembly. The gods and goddesses gathered together in their assembly hall and began to discuss what to do.

Thor sat restlessly as the Aesir hemmed and hawed. To him, the solution was simple. "Freyja, just put on a bridal dress and let me take you to Jötunheim," he said. "We'll marry you off to Thrym and he'll give me back my hammer!"

But Freyja wrinkled her nose in disdain at this suggestion. She imagined herself, dressed as a bride, riding with Thor in his chariot drawn by goats.

"And have everyone think that we've eloped?" Freyja asked. "I think not, Thor!"

But the watchman of the Aesir, Heimdall, banged his fist on the table with a grin on his face.

"I have a good idea!" he cried. "Let's send a decoy. Thor, why don't you go as the bride?"

"What!?" boomed Thor, as Loki broke into laughter beside him. "And have everyone think that I, Thor, am one for cross-dressing!?" His beard bristled and he puffed up his mighty chest in a heroic way. "I refuse."

"I'll go as the bridesmaid!" Loki offered.

The Aesir agreed that this was the best idea they could come up with, and so they dressed a begrudging Thor as a bride. They draped him in the wedding dress, hung the wedding keys at his side, and let the bridal veil fall over his eyes. And, as a final touch, Freyja put her sparking amber necklace around his neck.

"A spitting image of me," Freyja said wryly, watching Thor's eyes burn with fury from behind the veil.

Loki then emerged, having assumed the shape of a woman. "Shall we?" she said.

Thor's two goats were harnessed to his chariot, and he and his shrewd-looking bridesmaid galloped off to giant-country. The hoofbeats of the goats shook the ground and lightning sparked from the wheels of the chariot as the two of them careened over land and sky.

Thor and Loki rode for eight days and nights, traveling deep into the mountains of Jötunheim that bordered the rim of the world.

And, on the ninth day, Thrym saw them coming over the curve of a mountain. He turned to his men and grinned. "Look alive, boys!" he said. "It's time to spread straw on the benches and prepare the wedding feast! The Aesir have brought Njord's daughter, Freyja, to be my wife!"

Thrym's men scrambled to prepare the wedding feast, while he rubbed his hands together with glee.

"I have gold-horned cows walking in my fields and jet-black oxen in all their resplendency! I have troves of treasure and heaps of other precious luxuries! The only thing I don't have is the beautiful and wise Freyja. Only she is missing from the picture!"

When Thor's chariot landed, an extravagant wedding feast was thrown in Thrym's hall. The giant-king watched as his bride consumed one whole ox and eight salmon before downing three caskets of mead plus all the little delicacies made especially for the women.

"Goodness, Freyja, wherever did you get such an appetite!?" Thrym remarked.

The bride's clever-looking maid turned to look at the giant-king. "My lady was so eager to come to Jötunheim that she ate nothing for eight days!" she said. "But now she's here before you, Thrym, she has nothing but a voracious appetite."

Thrym took a moment to think about this before grinning, then leaned over to kiss his wife. But no sooner had he drawn back the veil in front of her eyes than he staggered backward in shock.

"Freyja, my love, why are your eyes so fierce?" he cried. "It's as though fires burn within them!"

The bride's clever-looking maid peered at the giant-king. "That's because my lady hasn't slept a wink for the past eight nights," she said. "She couldn't bear to lie down unless she was beside you!"

"Oh, Freyja, I had no idea you were taken by such love sickness," Thrym replied. "... But why does Freyja not speak to me herself?"

The bride's clever-looking maid grinned. "Why, it's because Freyja has not said a word for eight days and nights," she said. "For nothing escapes her but moans of desire when she does!"

And upon hearing this, Thrym could wait no longer. "That's it!" he cried. "Bring out the hammer and let's consecrate the bride! It's time for us to be wed as one!"

From the other room, two giants brought out Thor's hammer, carrying it across the hall and setting it upon the bride's lap.

Thor's heart laughed in his chest and his courage soared as he grasped the mighty hammer and raised it above his head, the veil falling from his head to reveal his true identity.

"Wait, you're not Freyja!" Thrym cried with horror.

Thor brought his hammer down upon the dining hall table so hard that it splintered into pieces. He then proceeded to slaughter every last giant in Thrym's estate, including Thrym himself.

Bloodied and grinning, Thor and Loki loaded the chariot with gold and goods before taking off into the countryside. The wheels blazed and thunder and lighting boomed and crashed all around them, and there was such a commotion that the Aesir knew that Thor had succeeded in getting his hammer back.

THOR AND LOKI JOURNEY TO GEIRROD'S COURTS

One of Thor's many escapades with Loki, the story of Thor and Loki journeying to Geirrod's courts, takes the two of them deep into Jötunheim without Thor's hammer. There, Thor is helped by Grid, the mother of Vidarr, to defeat Geirrod, a crafty giant.

It all began one day when Loki had borrowed Freyja's feathered cloak in order to enjoy a flight. He flew into Jötunheim and there found the courts of a giant named Geirrod, who absolutely loathed the Aesir, especially Thor.

Loki, in the shape of a bird, landed in one of the windows of Geirrod's hall to survey what was going on. But the giant-king spotted him and bellowed: "Why is that falcon sitting on the windowsill? Get him down from there at once!"

So Geirrod's men began to stack up boxes and chairs in order to reach the bird, swearing and cursing, until finally someone brought in a ladder.

Loki thought this was all very amusing and watched with an unconcerned gaze, knowing he could fly off as soon as Geirrod's men got close. But as he spread his wings, he found that his feet were stuck to the windowsill. Loki panicked as he was snatched up by Geirrod's men and brought before the giant-king.

Geirrod looked into the falcon's eyes and saw that there was a person in there. "Who are you?" he demanded. "Reveal yourself to me!"

Loki remained silent. So, in order to make him talk, Geirrod ordered for him to be locked in a chest for three months without any food or drink.

When Loki was released, Geirrod once again demanded that he speak and reveal who he was.

"Alright, I'll tell you!" Loki cried. "I'm Loki of the Aesir, and I want you to let me go! Please, I'll do anything!"

"Then bring Thor to me," said Geirrod. "But make sure he leaves his hammer and his belt of strength at home!"

So a very hungry and weak Loki hobbled out of Geirrod's courts and flew back to Asgard, where he ate an enormous meal and drank gallons of mead. Feeling a hundred times better, he set off to find Thor.

"Oh Thor!" Loki said, knocking on the doors of his hall.

Thor answered. "What brings you here Loki?" he asked. "It's been a few months since I've seen you!"

"I was at my friend Geirrod's courts," Loki said. "For three months I spent the time feasting and drinking and debauching like you wouldn't believe!

I don't think I could even see the table because of how much food there was on it! There was fish, oxen, and wild boar, and we drank mead and ale straight out of the kegs. Even just mentioning it to you, I'm in half a mind to go back and eat some more!" Thor's mouth was watering as Loki spoke.

"Oh, and we also wrestled," Loki continued. "They're an argumentative bunch, Geirrod's men. Always looking for someone to tussle with. But I could easily throw most of them with one hand behind my back!"

"Well, now you have to show me to Geirrod's courts," said Thor, picking up his hammer.

"Ah! Ah! Ah!" said Loki, waving his finger. "Geirrod has a custom that no guest shall bring anything that would grant an unfair advantage! This means no weapons or strength-enhancing girdles!"

Thor looked at his hammer with consternation, but then thought about the wild boar and kegs of endless mead.

"If you say so," Thor said.

So he left his hammer and belt of strength behind.

The two of them set out for Jötunheim on foot, eventually coming to the hall of Vidarr's mother, Grid, where they stopped for the evening.

Grid was a friendly giantess, and when she heard where Thor was going, she shook her head.

"Geirrod isn't some merrymaking numbskull," she warned. "He's cunning and very strong, and you shouldn't be caught in his hall without weapons to defend yourself. Here, I have a magic staff, a belt of strength, and an iron mitt. Take these, and use them when you contend with the giant."

Thor thanked her and took the magic staff, belt of strength, and iron mitt with him when he set out on his journey with Loki the following morning.

Eventually, Thor and Loki came to a river, which they had to wade across. But halfway across, the river began to rise.

Thor dug Grid's magic staff into the river bed to steady himself, while Loki gripped the belt of strength to prevent the current from carrying him away.

Thor looked up the river and saw a giantess straddling it. She was one of Geirrod's daughters, named Gialp, saying an enchantment to make the water rise. Seeing this, Thor scooped up a large rock and hurled it at the giantess, who screamed and ran off when it hit her.

"A river must be stemmed at its source," Thor said.

Thor and Loki drifted by a rowan tree, which they used to pull themselves out of the river and onto the other bank. After squeezing the water out of their clothes and hair, they continued on to Geirrod's courts.

The welcome Thor and Loki received was hardly hospitable. The giants met them with cold expressions, and when they were shown to their quarters, they found that this was a goat shed, inside which there was only a single chair.

Thor sat in the chair, but, as soon as he did so, the chair began to rise rapidly toward the ceiling. Thor held out Grid's magic staff and pushed it hard into the rafters of the shed—so hard that the chair came crashing down.

Thor heard a crunching sound and terrible screams, and looked down to see two giantesses pinned beneath the stool. They were Geirrod's daughters, Gialp and Greip, who had attempted to crush Thor against the ceiling but only broke their backs as a result.

As Gialp and Greip hobbled out, another giant appeared and told Thor that Geirrod had invited them to the hall to participate in some games.

"Finally!" said Thor.

He and Loki entered the hall and saw Geirrod standing at the other end in front of a roaring fire with a pair of iron tongs in his hands.

Using the tongs, Geirrod took a flaming bolt from the fire and hurled it straight at Thor. But Thor caught the bolt with the iron mitt, just as Geirrod hid behind one of the hall pillars.

Furious, Thor threw the bolt back at Geirrod so hard that it smashed through the pillar, the giant-king, the wall, and finally into the ground, where it lay smoldering. The giant, meanwhile, fell down dead.

"I guess we're not going to find a meal here," said Thor.

So he and Loki left Geirrod's courts as hungry as before.

THOR AND LOKI VISIT UTGARD-LOKI

A story in which Loki and Thor visit a strange magician named Utgard-Loki in Jötunheim and are tested through various challenges and contests. The humbling events that ensue are filled with strife, deception, and trickery.

Thor and Loki were roaming across the land, traveling over hills and mountains in Thor's chariot, when dusk began to fall. Just then, they came to the house of a peasant and his family, and were given shelter for the night.

"I'm very sorry," the peasant said to them. "There isn't any food we can offer you for tonight."

"There's no need for concern!" Thor replied. "We can just slaughter my goats!"

The peasant looked stricken at this. "But your chariot!" he said. "You don't have any other animals that will draw it!"

"Well, of course not," said Thor. "Because my goats will draw it in the morning! As long as we throw all the bones back onto their skins without harming any of them, I'll be able to resurrect the goats good as new."

So the goats were slaughtered and roasted over the fire. They made for a splendid meal, and as everyone finished picking the meat off the bones, they tossed them back onto the goatskins, which Thor had spread over the ground.

The farmer's two children were a boy and girl, named Thjalfi and Roskva. Thjalfi was sitting next to Loki on the benches, and Loki leaned over to him and said:

"A fine meal indeed, but it's a darn shame we can't get at any of the marrow in the bones. It sure looks tasty!"

Thjalfi looked at the ham-bone he was holding, and slyly, he took his knife and split the bone down the center, so he could get at the marrow in the middle.

The next morning, Thor got up just before daybreak and waved his hammer Mjolnir over the goatskins, blessing them, so the goats would rise good as new. However, he noticed one of them was now lame in one leg.

Thor's brows sank over his eyes, which blazed with a fiery anger in his skull. "Someone didn't treat the bones carefully!" he growled, clenching his hammer so tightly that his knuckles turned white.

The peasant, upon hearing this, fell upon his knees. "Please, forgive us!" he said. "Allow me to compensate you for the trouble!"

On seeing how terrified the man was, Thor calmed down and accepted the peasant's two children, Thjalfi and Roskva, as repayment. They have been his attendants ever since.

Since the goats could no longer pull the chariot, Thor left them behind, and he, Loki, Thjalfi, and Roskva continued onward to Jötunheim, crossing the sea and landing upon the shore, where they were met by a huge, dark forest.

The four of them walked on through the immense forest until night began to fall once more, but they came across neither path nor settlement, no matter which way they turned.

Just before the sky turned pitch-black, they came across a strange structure with an entrance as wide as it was tall.

There they settled for the night, but at around midnight, the four of them awoke suddenly to what seemed to be a huge, shuddering earthquake.

Thor clenched his hammer fearfully, the rest of his companions looking equally frightened, and slowly they all crept outside, where there was a great deal of grumbling and rumbling going on.

Once outside, they found the source of all the noise—an enormous giant, sleeping right next to the structure they had previously been in.

Thor was so astounded by the giant's massive size that he was too terrified to strike him with his hammer.

Soon the giant awoke and saw the four of them standing before him. "It would seem I have guests," he said.

"And just who are you?" asked Thor.

"I am Skrymir," the giant replied. "Though I hardly need to ask for your names. You're clearly Thor of the Aesir, traveling with Loki and your two companions. But what were you four doing, making off with my glove?"

The giant reached over and picked up the structure Thor and the rest had been sleeping in, and they saw that the hall was none other than a giant mitten.

"Would you like to travel together?" Skrymir asked. "I'd be more than happy to carry your goods for you."

They all agreed, and after breakfast, Skrymir placed their food bag in his knapsack and began to walk. He took such long strides that Thor, Loki, and the two children had to run to keep up.

That night, as they made camp under a large oak tree, Skrymir said to Thor: "I'm going to sleep early tonight, but you're welcome to take your food from my knapsack." Then he rolled over and went to sleep, snoring loudly.

Thor got up and took Skrymir's knapsack, but no matter how much he tried, he couldn't seem to get the knot undone. No amount of pulling or finagling made it any looser. Soon he got fed up with it all and flew into a rage, picking up his hammer and bringing it hard down on Skrymir's sleeping head.

Skrymir awoke, blinking. "I could swear that a falling leaf awoke me just now," he said, and then he looked at Thor and asked if they had finished eating.

Shocked that the blow of his hammer had done nothing and wanting to save face, Thor said, "We were just getting ready to sleep." He, Loki, Thjalfi, and

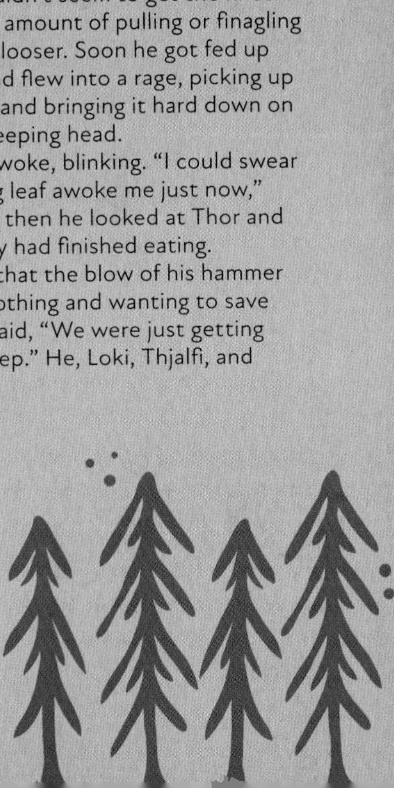

Roskva retired underneath a different oak tree, and they all struggled to fall asleep for fear of Skrymir's imperviousness to Thor's hammer Mjolnir.

But midnight eventually rolled around, and Skrymir was making such a racket with his snoring that Thor became increasingly irritated. He got up and swung his hammer as hard as he could at Skrymir's sleeping head, feeling it sink deep within his face.

But Skrymir blinked his eyes awake and said, "What's the matter this time? Did an acorn just fall on my head? And what are you doing, Thor? Shouldn't you be sound asleep?"

Thor mumbled that he was simply returning from going to the bathroom, resolving that Skrymir would not open his eyes the third time he struck.

Thor waited until the giant was asleep once more, and then he charged at him and swung his hammer down with all his might. But Skrymir simply awoke from his slumbers yet again.

"I suppose a twig landed on me," the giant said. "Anyway, it's morning and I'll be heading north now. If you keep going east, you'll eventually reach Utgard-Loki and his settlement. But be warned: As large as you think I am, Utgard-Loki and his men are far bigger, and they don't take kindly to shows of arrogance from runts like yourselves." And then he gave Thor back his bag of food and headed northward toward the mountains.

Thor, Loki, Thjalfi, and Roskva continued on their way until eventually they came to a mighty stronghold in a flat expanse of land. It was so huge that they had to crane their necks just to look at it. They walked up to the massive gate, but try as they might, it would not budge, so instead they squeezed between the bars to let themselves in.

Fortunately, the mighty doors to the great longhall were propped open, and when they entered, they saw giants of impressive sizes sitting on the benches. Thor and his companions went up to their king, Utgard-Loki, who took his time to greet them, and when he finally did he gave them a cold, wicked grin.

"Is that little fellow Thor, I see?" he questioned. "You must be mightier than you look. What sort of feat can you do?"

"Feat?" Thor questioned

"Yes! A feat!" said Utgard-Loki. "You see, none may have a seat here in my feasting hall unless they can do something no one else can... and prove it! That's why you must show me your skills."

At the rear of the group was Loki, and hearing this, he spoke up:

"I know of a feat that I'm more than ready to demonstrate!" he said. "I bet there's no one here who can eat faster than I can!"

"That would be quite a feat indeed, if true," said Utgard-Loki. "Let's put it to the test! Logi! Come down from the benches please and prove yourself in an eating contest!"

And so the giant named Logi came onto the floor. He had orange hair as bright as a flame. Loki sat across from Logi, and a trencher filled with meat was placed between them.

"And... start!" commanded Utgard-Loki to the competitors.

Loki shoveled meat morsel after morsel into his mouth, leaving behind nothing but the bones. He and Logi met exactly in the middle of the trencher at exactly the same time."

"Logi is the winner!" Utgard-Loki pronounced. Loki looked and saw that Logi had eaten not only the meat off the bones, but the bones themselves and the trencher too.

"I have a feat I would like to try," said Thjalfi enthusiastically. "I would like to run a race against anyone you'll put me up against because I bet that no one here can run faster than me!"

"A noble feat," said Utgard-Loki. "Let's see if it holds up."

And from the benches he summoned a giant called Hugi. They all walked outside where there was an area of flat land, and a course was charted for them to run to a large tree and back.

"And... start!" commanded Utgard-Loki.

Thjalfi and Hugi bolted. Thjalfi ran quickly, but Hugi overtook him and was already running back to the finish line before Thjalfi had even reached the tree.

"You will have to do better than that if you want to win!" said Utgard-Loki. "Though it's true that you are the fastest visitor I've ever received."

Thjalfi and Hugi raced again, but even though Thjalfi ran even more swiftly, Hugi was still ahead of him and won.

"At this rate I'm not sure if you'll be able to win," Utgard-Loki said to the boy. "But we shall see what happens during the third race."

Unfortunately, Hugi won yet again, finishing before Thjalfi had even reached the halfway point. The race was decided and Hugi was declared the victor.

"And what feats will you be showing off, Thor?" Utgard-Loki asked.

Thor thought about this for a moment before declaring: "I'm more than willing to compete at a drinking contest with someone."

"Then a drinking contest it is!" said Utgard-Loki.

A drinking horn was brought out, and although it wasn't any bigger than most other horns, it was exceptionally long.

"Most would agree that a good drinker could drain the horn in one go, but some

finish it all in two," said Utgard-Loki. "But the man who can't finish it in three is not a man with a stomach for booze!"

So Thor took the horn and began to drink thirstily, downing the contents gulp after gulp. But when he lowered the horn and looked into it, the level of the liquid had barely changed at all.

"Not bad showmanship!" said Utgard-Loki. "Although I'm surprised at your moderation, Thor. I would have thought someone as mighty as you would have taken a greater swig. But I'm confident you'll finish it this time."

Thor made no reply, instead scowling darkly at the horn. He raised it to his lips once more, taking an even mightier draft. But when he lowered the horn and looked into it, it seemed to have gone down even less than before.

"What's the matter, Thor?" asked Utgard-Loki. "Why are you holding back? I'm beginning to think you're not as mighty as your reputation has led me to believe. If you can't finish it all on the third try... "

Angry at this, Thor braced his stance, and took from the horn the mightiest of all drinks, drinking and drinking until he was out of breath. He gasped, pulling the horn away, and looked inside it once more. The level had gone down more than before, but it was still quite full.

"It would appear you're not so great after all," said Utgard-Loki. "Would you like to try another contest? It seems you're getting nowhere with this one."

Thor gave the horn away and said, "Well, what sort of contest do you have in mind?"

Utgard-Loki thought about it for a moment, and then he replied, "The small lads of Utgard like to play a certain game of strength, though it may seem like no big deal for us grown men. The game is to see whether they can lift my cat up off the ground. I would never have thought of mentioning it, but seeing how winded you got during the last competition, then... "

"I'll do it," said Thor. Just as he spoke, a gray cat ran out onto the floor. It was quite large, but not so large that Thor thought he couldn't pick it up. So he rubbed his hands together, dug them underneath the cat's belly, and lifted it up. But the cat only stretched longer and longer, keeping all four of his paws on the floor even as his back was arched.

Thor lifted and grunted, reaching as high as he could, until one of the cat's paws came off the ground. But he could not lift the cat beyond that.

"It's just as I expected," Utgard-Loki said. "For the cat is, indeed, big and Thor is quite the runt compared to the rest of us!" At this, Thor became furious.

"Runt my boot!" he cried. "I bet no one here will say that after a fight with me!"

"I don't think anyone on the benches would demean themselves by fighting such a weak opponent," Utgard-Loki said. "But if it's a fight you want, it's a fight you'll get. Bring the old women to me, lads! Bring me my nurse, Elli!"

Soon, a little old lady hobbled forward.

"Elli, see that you give Thor a good wrestling match," Utgard-Loki said.

Thor knew it wasn't polite to tackle old women, so when the match began he intended to set her down gently. But when he tried to budge her from her spot, she didn't move. He wrestled harder, but she wrestled back, surprisingly strong despite her frail form. Or was Thor getting weaker? With every grapple he tried, he felt himself become more and more winded, until he fell to one knee.

"Enough!" cried Utgard-Loki. "Clearly, there's no use issuing you with more challenges! It seems your strength and reputation are greatly overstated."

It was late by now, so Utgard-Loki showed Thor, Loki, Thjalfi, and Roskva to their quarters. Exhausted from the day's events, they all fell straight to sleep without having demonstrated any feats in order to earn dinner that night.

In the morning, Thor and his three companions rose and were just about to leave when Utgard-Loki appeared, saying he had prepared a table for them. Surprised, but not unwelcoming of the sudden hospitality, the four of them enjoyed a hearty meal.

When they finally left, Utgard-Loki accompanied them down the road. Once Utgard was in the distance, he stopped.

"It's time I told you the truth, now that we have left my fortress," he said in a grave voice. "And I swear I would never let you into it to begin with, had I known you had such great and terrible strength within you."

Thor frowned suspiciously. "What do you mean?" he said.

"I've deceived you with many illusions," Utgard-Loki admitted. "The first time

was when we met in the forest, and I was the giant called Skrymir. You remember the knapsack you couldn't untie? Well, I had tied it with a troll-knot, so it couldn't be undone by anything other than magic. You were so furious that when you brought your hammer down upon my head, I had only a fraction of a moment to pull a mountain between us. See those three deep valleys in the distant mountain range? Those were created by the blows of your hammer." Thor looked into the distance and indeed saw the three valleys Utgard-Loki had created.

"I also blinded you all with troll-magic during the games we played," Utgard-Loki continued. "Loki's eating partner was Logi, but Logi's true form is wildfire, and nothing consumes faster or more thoroughly than wildfire. Thjalfi ran against Hugi, but Hugi's true form is a thought... and who can race faster than a thought? And, as for you, Thor, you didn't know this, but the drinking horn I gave you was connected to the ocean, and you drank so mightily that all the waves in the world sank back from their shorelines!"

Thor's head was reeling just thinking about all this.

"And as for the cat you lifted," said Utgard-Loki, "it was none other than Jormungand, the Midgard Serpent! You scared us all tremendously when we saw you lifting it so high over the mountains and clouds that it touched the sky, with its tail barely skimming the earth! And when you wrestled the old woman, Elli, it was no less than miraculous that you only fell on one knee, for Elli is Old Age herself, and there isn't anyone that Old Age can't bring down... And now that I've told you all this, I swear that if I can have it my way, we shall never cross paths again. Goodbye, Thor."

Thor was so furious that his eyes flashed. He took up his hammer and lifted it high, but when he blinked, the giant had vanished. He looked out at the

landscape and saw that his stronghold had also gone.

Unable to find any sign of the giant, Thor, Loki, Thjalfi, and Roskva turned away from that landscape, and made their way out of Jötunheim and back to Asgard.

MORAL OF THE STORY

This story appears to have been told to children frustrated by being unable to perform the same feats as older kids and adults. It places Thor, the mightiest of the Aesir, in similar predicaments when he visits a hall full of enormous giants much bigger than himself... only to learn it was all an illusion—and Thor's strength terrified them all. This would have helped restore children's sense of competency as they grew up.

THOR FETCHES A CAULDRON AND GOES FISHING

The story of Thor going fishing is an amalgamation of a few different tales and tropes. The original tale, *Hymiskviða*, uses an abundance of kennings, or poetic turns of phrase, to describe people and things. It also features Tyr as Thor's traveling companion, but this may have not been the case in the original story.

Long, long ago, Odin, Tyr, Thor, and a number of the Aesir went out hunting during the winter season. They were lucky in their hunt and ended up bagging some wild birds. They built a fire in a small grove and roasted the birds over a spit. But just as they were devouring the meat like a pack of hungry wolves, they found themselves craving the flavor of ale. However, none of them had any kettles in which they could brew it.

Driven by this thirst, Thor and the others huddled in a circle around Odin as he consulted a cup that held some long sticks. The Allfather drew one of the sticks, then another, and then another, gazing at the runes drawn on their ends. He considered these for a moment before looking at his men and saying, "The giant-king of the sea, Aegir, has an abundance of kettles. We'll find him at the shore by the cliffs."

"And how are we supposed to persuade Aegir to part with those kettles?" asked Thor.

"I have a better idea," Odin replied.

So together they rode to the edge of the land, where they found Aegir, just as the lot-cup had said. Odin looked at him sharply with his one eye.

"Aegir!" he said. "I hear you own a great number of fine kettles. We've been looking for a mead-hall where we can drink and make merry, so surely you'd be more than happy to help your neighbors throw their drinking-feasts, yes?"

Aegir saw through Odin's prodding and grimaced at the sudden predicament the wily Allfather had put him in. He knew it was unwise to refuse; if he did, Odin would take the opportunity to call him inhospitable. Thor's presence also offered no comfort, for the giant-slayer stood there with barely contained contempt, his red hair bristling and his hand grasping the hilt of Mjolnir.

Aegir scratched his seafoam-white beard and thought hard about ways to get back at the gods.

"Yes, I'd be more than happy to… if only my kettles were big enough," he replied. "It's true that I have many, but they're all quite small, only fit for little trolls and small creatures living at the bottom of the sea. But if your son Thor, the strongest of your men, could find a brewing vessel large enough for me to make ale for all of you, then I would be more than happy to host drinking nights for the Aesir."

The gods rode off, considering where they could find such a large kettle.

Back in Asgard, Thor searched high and low, but came up short every time. He was about to return to Aegir, just to bash him on the head, when the one-handed god, Tyr, approached him in private.

"I have an answer to our problems, Thor," Tyr said. "My father, the giant Hymir, has a massive cauldron, stout, well-built, and a whole league deep."

Thor perked up at this. "Do you think we can get a hold of it?" he asked.

"Yes," said Tyr, "but we will have to use trickery to do it!"

So that very day, they set out from Asgard in Thor's chariot drawn by goats, crossing the Elivagar rivers and beyond until they arrived at the abode of an elf named Egill, whom Thor tasked with watching his goats.

Thor and Tyr then continued on foot to Hymir's hall. Tyr knocked on the door and was greeted by his grandmother, a terrible, ugly troll with over nine hundred heads. But Tyr's mother was also there, dressed in gold and white. She greeted them warmly: "Tyr! Thor! What brings you here?" she asked.

The two travelers explained their quest, and she replied, "Hymir may let you have it, but I must warn you that my husband has a foul temper and isn't fond of unexpected guests. He may become enraged if he sees you. Hide behind that pillar over there, so he doesn't see you right away when he returns."

Thor and Tyr grumbled about this—especially Thor, who hated hiding from giants—but they did what they were told. No sooner had they hunkered down behind the pillar than Hymir returned home from hunting. Icicles broke from his frozen beard and clattered upon the ground as he entered the abode.

"Welcome home, Hymir!" his wife said. "I hope you're in a good mood. Guess who's come to visit? Your son, Tyr, and a fellow kinsman. They are waiting to greet you from behind the pillar."

Hymir shot such an intense look at the pillar that it snapped under his cutting stare. The crossbeam above collapsed, and the eight kettles hanging from it crashed to the floor, breaking into pieces as they did so. But a ninth, a massive and sturdy cauldron, hit the floor unscathed.

Hymir regretted this decision as soon as he saw who his son had brought with him—Thor, slayer of giants. "Let's make a meal for our guests," he said, knowing full well that Thor's hatred for giants could be tempered by a good meal. Hymir had three whole oxen beheaded and prepared in the cooking pit, two of which Thor ate entirely himself. The last oxen was split between Tyr and the rest of the house.

"We'll have to go hunting in the morning if you expect to have anything to eat tomorrow," Hymir said to Thor bitterly.

"Let's row out to sea and catch something," Thor replied. "Could you provide the bait?"

Hymir shook his head. "If you want bait, you can get some from the herd of wild oxen," he snorted. "If you dare... "

However, Thor wasn't deterred, and the next morning he went to the forest where the wild oxen roamed. He came across one as black as pitch, and without hesitation, he grabbed the animal by the horns and snapped its head clean off.

Hymir snorted upon seeing Thor carry back the head of an ox. "Hardly impressive," he said. "It would seem that what you accomplish when busy is worse than what you accomplish standing still."

Thor wordlessly took the ox head onto Hymir's boat, and the two of them rowed out to sea. When they got a way out, Hymir began baiting his line.

"Let's row out farther," Thor said, but Hymir shook his head.

"This suits me just fine," he said, casting his line.

Soon the giant hooked a catch and hauled in two enormous whales.

Thor, meanwhile, baited his fishing hook with the head of the ox and cast it out to sea. The head sank all the way down to the bottom of the ocean, and Thor felt a mighty tug as something massive swallowed it whole. He wrenched his line, and the water began to boil. The beast that emerged was none other than Jormungand, the giant serpent who circled the Earth.

Thor wrestled the serpent's head up to the gunwale before striking it with his hammer. Crack! The blow reverberated all the way back to land and across the rocky shores, shaking the Earth.

The Midgard Serpent roared, the hook dislodging from its jaws, before it sank back under the raging waves.

Hymir quaked at this feat of strength, but didn't show it to Thor. Instead, he fell into a foul mood as the two of them rowed back to shore with their catch.

When they finally landed, the giant asked Thor, "Will you do half the work, either by carrying the whales to the farmhouse or securing the boat?"

Thor didn't say a word, but instead pulled the boat with the whales, oars, bilge bucket, and bilgewater onto the shore. Then he hoisted the two sea-beasts over his shoulders and carried them back to the farm, with Hymir trailing empty-handed behind him.

Tyr's grandmother cooked the whales, and all of them ate heartily that evening.

Tyr then took the opportunity to mention the cauldron: "Surely you wouldn't mind giving it to us," he said to his father. "After all, Thor has earned the favor with all his feats of strength today."

"There's only one feat of strength that'll make me hand over my cauldron," Hymir grumbled, "and that is if you can break my crystal goblet. Do that, and I'll hand you the cauldron."

Thor threw the crystal goblet as hard as he could at one of the hall's pillars, but it simply pierced through the wood and landed whole on the other side.

Tyr's mother leaned in close to Thor. "Strike it hard on Hymir's head after he's eaten his fill," she whispered. "His skull is harder than any crystal goblet!"

So once the giant had settled down to relax after dinner, Thor picked up the goblet again and smashed it hard upon Hymir's skull. The goblet shattered and Hymir groaned. "I have lost many treasures today," he said. "First my goblet, and now my cauldron, both of which I need to make booze. Never again will I be able to say, 'Ale, now you are brewed!' You may have won yourself a cauldron today, boys, but let's see how you feel about carrying it out!"

Tyr tried to lift the cauldron twice, and twice it failed to budge. But Thor seized it by the rim and swung it upon his head. It was so heavy that his feet sank right through the floor of the hall, and so large that the handles banged against his heels.

He and Tyr made their way out the door and walked for a while before Thor looked behind him. He saw a whole troop of multiheaded trolls and giants flowing from the crevices between the rock, burning hot with a fiery rage. They were led by an angry Hymir.

Thor set the cauldron down and pulled out his hammer, and with several dozen strikes of Mjolnir, he killed every single giant attacking him.

Eventually they arrived back at Egill's place, where they loaded the cauldron onto Thor's chariot and drove off. But one of Thor's goats was limping badly with a lame leg as a result of their prior adventures visiting Utgard-Loki.

Thor and Tyr finally reached Asgard where they received a hero's welcome. The cauldron was brought to Aegir, who marveled that the Aesir had accomplished such a task. He didn't dare go back on his word, so he threw a fantastic feast for the Aesir and hosted such a feast every winter thereafter.

THOR OUTWITS A DWARF

Found in the *Poetic Edda*, the poem Alvíssmál tells the tale of how Thor interfered with a dwarf's plans to marry his daughter, Thrud. It's a rare story of Thor using his brains rather than brawn to solve a problem... and not without success!

Thor was awake and out for a walk in the hours just before dawn. Along the way, he passed a squat little dwarf who seemed far more cheerful than usual for his kind.

"What has you in such a fine mood?" Thor asked him, and the dwarf gave him a toothy grin.

"Why, I'm getting married!" said the dwarf. "To none other than the most beautiful Thrud!"

Thor was about to bellow with rage upon hearing his daughter's name when he remembered the time of night and everyone sleeping in nearby Asgard. He cleared his throat, composing himself, and looked down at the dwarf.

"And what sort of creature are you, thinking you can get away with something like that?" Thor asked. "You hardly look fit for a bride."

"My name is Alvis or All-Wise," the dwarf said. "I live below the earth and have my dwelling under a rock. I've come up here now only to take Thrud's hand in marriage, and I shall let no one interfere with our vows!"

"Well, I shall interfere!" Thor retorted. "I have the most authority in this matter as her father, after all. I wasn't at home when she was promised to you."

"And you are... ?" questioned Alvis.

"Thor is my name, son of Odin," Thor said. "And only with my consent will you be able to seek my daughter's hand in marriage."

"Then I'll strive to gain it," Alvis replied. "For I can't imagine going without such a fine woman! What are your terms?"

Thor scratched his beard, looking at the blue dawn on the horizon. He didn't want to wake everyone up by bashing the lovesick dwarf over the head with Mjolnir, so instead he thought about what his own father would do.

"If you're truly as wise as you say, then I ask that you tell me everything in all the worlds that I wish to know," Thor said. "Only then can you seek my daughter's hand in marriage."

"Gladly," the dwarf replied.

Thor settled upon a rock and thought about his first question.

Said Thor:

"Tell me, Alvis, how is the earth referred to in each world?"

Said Alvis:

"It's called 'earth' by men, 'ground' by the Aesir, and the Vanir call it 'ways.' The giants call it 'splendid-green,' the elves call it 'the growing one,' and the powers in the realms above call it 'loam.'"

Said Thor:

"Tell me, Alvis, how is the sky referred to in each world?"

Said Alvis:

"It's called 'sky' by men, 'planet-home' by the gods, and 'wind-weaver' by the

Vanir. The giants call it 'the world above,' the elves call it 'the lovely roof,' and the dwarves call it 'the dripping hall.'"

Said Thor:

"Tell me, Alvis, how is the moon referred to in each world?"

Said Alvis:

"It's called 'moon' by men, 'ball' by the gods, and in Helheim it's called 'the whirling wheel.' The giants call it 'the hastener,' the dwarves call it 'the shiner,' and the elves call it 'counter of years.'"

Said Thor:

"Tell me, Alvis, how is the sun referred to in each world?"

Said Alvis:

"It's called 'sun' by men, 'sunshine' by the gods, and the dwarves call it 'Dvalin's plaything.' The giants call it 'everglow,' the elves call it 'the lovely wheel,' and the sons of the Aesir call it 'all-shining.'"

On and on this continued, with Thor asking questions and Alvis answering in kind. What is sea called? What is fire called? What are wood, barley, and ale called? But after the dwarf had answered all these questions, the sun finally cracked over the horizon.

"I'll admit I haven't come across another being who knows more than you," said Thor. "But I've duped you, dwarf. The sun is now shining, and ground-dwelling creatures like yourself fade under its brightness. My daughter shall not elope with you."

Thor stood up from where he had been seated and went on his way, for there was no answer the dwarf could give; he had turned to stone in the sunlight.

THOR FIGHTS THE GIANT HRUNGNIR

Likely aimed at little children, this story potentially came about as a way to encourage them not to throw whetstones across the floor, using a narrative to explain that this gives Thor (and probably also the parents) a splitting headache.

One day, Odin burst through the gates of Asgard, riding on his horse Sleipnir, followed quickly in pursuit by a giant named Hrungnir. The two had bet on a race to see whose horse was faster, Odin's or Hrungnir's golden steed, and the giant had got so caught up in the race that he didn't realize they had passed through Asgard's gates.

Not wanting to cause a stir when he was at a disadvantage, Hrungnir took the drinks offered to him by the valkyries, but soon he began to boast hideously.

"I will remove Valhalla and take it back with me to Jötunheim!" Hrungnir proclaimed. "And Asgard I will destroy and bury in the rubble, and kill all of the gods! Oh, but I will make sure to take Freyja and Sif home with me, that I will!"

And after those mighty words, only Freyja dared to bring him more drinks.

Soon the Aesir grew tired of Hrungnir's proud claims and called out Thor's name. Thor appeared at the doors of Valhalla immediately, his eyes burning with fiery anger and with his hammer Mjolnir raised above his head.

"Who let a giant in here?" Thor roared. "And why is Freyja serving him drinks as if this were a dinner party?"

Hrungnir looked at Thor without a shred of kindness in his eyes. "Why, it was Odin himself who invited me in for a drink!" the giant replied. "I'm under his protection!"

And hearing this, Thor's eyes flashed. "You're going to regret accepting the protection of Odin before you leave here," he growled.

But Hrungnir scoffed. "You'd be a scoundrel man to kill me now, when I'm unarmed," he said. "Demonstrate your honor and fight a duel against me later!"

Thor was more than eager to agree to a duel, for no one had ever dared to challenge him to one before. "You have a deal," he said.

Hrungnir then rode back to Jötunheim, and soon word of his duel with Thor spread far and wide.

The giants were concerned. Hrungnir was the biggest and strongest of the giants, but despite this, his kin felt there was a great risk in fighting Thor, for if Hrungnir lost they could no longer count on him to protect them.

So just before the battle, the giants met on the field where the duel between Thor and Hrungnir was to take place and built a man made of clay, who was nine leagues high and three leagues wide, but they couldn't find a heart that was big enough for him. Eventually, the giants took a heart out of a mare, but it beat faintly, as hearts go.

By the time Thor arrived, the clay giant was quite terrified, and, as the story goes, he even wet himself.

Hrungnir's heart, however, was made of stone, as were his head and his shield.

He had a whetstone for a weapon, which he rested against his shoulder as Thor stepped before him.

"Consider this day your last!" said Thor.

The duel commenced, but, at that moment, Thor's man Thjalfi ran forward to Hrungnir and said:

"Giant, you have let your guard down! Even though you have your stone shield in front of you, Thor has seen you and he's traveling fast through the ground below and will strike your feet!"

At this, Hrungnir quickly threw his shield upon the ground. But Thor charged after him and his hammer collided with Hrugnir's whetstone, which broke in two.

One piece fell to the ground, and from it came all the whetstone rocks in the world. The second piece lodged itself in Thor's head. Shouting in agony, Thor

brought his mighty hammer down on the giant's skull and smashed it to pieces. Hrungnir's body toppled forward and fell onto Thor, trapping him beneath.

In the meantime, Thjalfi had done away with the man made out of clay. Seeing Thor trapped beneath Hrungnir's body, he rushed over to him and attempted to lift the giant's leg from him. But he had no luck. All the Aesir tried, but none could budge Hrungnir's body.

But then Magni, Thor's three-year-old son who he'd had with the giantess Jarnsaxa arrived, and the little boy lifted the leg from his father with ease.

Thor stood up, overjoyed with his son, and proclaimed proudly that he would grow up to be fine and powerful.

"I have also decided to give you the horse Gullfaxi, who once belonged to Hrungnir!" Thor bellowed.

Another problem remained, however, and it was giving Thor a headache. When he returned home, Thor fetched a sorceress called Groa to help him remove the whetstone that was stuck in his head.

As Groa chanted her spells over Thor, the whetstone began to dislodge. He was so delighted that he gave her news of her husband, Aurvandil, as a way of repaying her. Thor had waded south across the Elivagar rivers from Jötunheim carrying Aurvandil in a basket on his back. He told Groa that it would not be long now before Aurvandil was home.

Groa was so overjoyed at the news and all the chatting that she forgot every one of her spells, so the whetstone remained stuck in Thor's head.

Now, every time we throw whetstones across the room, it makes the one in Thor's head rattle, giving him a throbbing headache. And this is why we should always be very careful to treat our whetstones well.

THOR ARGUES WITH GRAYBEARD THE FERRYMAN

A later tale, the story of Graybeard the ferryman features Odin donning the disguise of a ferryman and testing the mind (and temperament) of his son Thor. Meanwhile, Thor is simply trying to cross a fjord.

Thor was returning from Jötunheim, traveling westward back to Asgard down an unfamiliar path. He whistled as he carried a basket of food on his back, until he came across a fjord cutting the land in half like a river.

Thor squinted, shielding his eyes from the sun, and saw on the other side an old ferryman reclining in his boat. He was looking bored.

Unknown to Thor, the Allfather, Odin, had disguised himself as the ferryman.

"Hullo!" Thor bellowed. "Who's that fine fellow standing at the other side of the water?"

"Who is that sarcastic bumpkin hollering from over the gulf!" the ferryman replied, unamused by Thor's sense of humor.

"You're a ferryman, yes?" said Thor. "If you take me across the fjord, I'll repay you with a morning's breakfast! I just had my fill of herring and oatmeal before I left on my journey, and this basket I carry has some excellent food inside!"

But the ferryman scoffed from the other side of the fjord, rolling his eyes in utter contempt.

"You seem so proud of that," he said. "Sharing your meal with me and not paying for transportation across the fjord. Do you know when you'll get your next meal? I bet your mother is dead."

Thor furrowed his brow and thought about it. "That would be terrible news for a lot of people, if my mother were dead," he said—because his mother was the very Earth herself.

"Do you even have three good farms to your name?" the ferryman cried. "You're walking barefoot and you are dressed all in rags!"

Thor pouted at this. "Enough of that!" he said. "Bring your boat over here, so I can get across! By the way, whose boat are you in charge of?"

"My employer's name is Hildolf," the ferryman replied. "And he's an esteemed warrior, who is very wise, and he lives in the nearby Rathsey's Fjord. He ordered me not to ferry hooligans like bandits and horse thieves across the water, but only upstanding men and those I clearly recognize. And you, sir, look like a hooligan, nor can I say I've ever seen the likes of you before!"

"Why, I would tell you my name even if I were an outlaw!" Thor boomed, immediately furious. "I'm the son of Odin, brother of Meili, father of Magni, and the mightiest of the Aesir—you are speaking to Thor! And now what I would like to know is, who are you?"

"I am Graybeard," the ferryman replied. "And I have little reason to hide my name."

"Why would you hide it anyway?" Thor

asked. “It’s not as if there is a dispute between us.”

But Graybeard scoffed. “Dispute or not, I still wouldn’t mingle with the likes of you!” he said. “Not unless I’d be struck dead if I didn’t!”

Now Thor was very angry. He pulled out his hammer and started to make his way to the water, only to stop and think about getting wet. He didn’t want to step into the freezing cold water.

“You great crybaby!” he shouted to Graybeard, deciding to pace the banks instead. “I’ll make you pay for your mockery if I get across!”

“I’ll be here waiting if you do!” Graybeard shouted back to Thor. “You haven’t fought a tougher man since Hrungnir died!”

Thor pounded his chest with one fist. “So you know a thing or two about fighting then, yes?” he retorted.

And with that, the two of them launched into an exchange of back-and-forth boasts, bragging about their various accomplishments as warriors.

Thor said to Graybeard: “Yes, I fought against Hrungnir, a giant as wide as he was tall, with a head made of stone and a heart to match! He was fierce, but I was fiercer, and I knocked him flat with my hammer. And what, may I ask, have you done, Graybeard?

Said Graybeard: “I was out with the boys for five long winters, fighting, plundering, and chasing women! Those girls were clever, yes, but I was cleverer, and I woo’d them all in the end! And what, Thor, have you done?”

Said Thor: “I killed the giant Thiazi and tossed his eyes into the sky where they shine as stars each night. Now all mankind can look to the sky and see the greatest of my deeds! And what, Graybeard, have you done?

Said Graybeard: “I enchanted witches with terrible love spells and woo’d them away from their husbands. I received a magic wand from a giant who gave it to me as a gift, and I used it to steal away his reason!”

“That was a dirty trick you pulled, repaying his gift like that!” cried Thor, breaking the rhythm of the banter.

“One oak tree thrives when another’s bark is stripped,” Graybeard said plainly.

“In this world, it’s every man for himself. And what have you done, Thor?”

Back and forth Thor and Graybeard went on like this, with Thor recounting all the giants he had slain and Graybeard recalling all the wars he’d fought.

But Thor was quickly becoming frustrated—words were not his usual weapon of combat, and he was finding it increasingly difficult to find replies when Graybeard was so quick with his own.

Very soon, Thor got fed up. “Where did you get all these smartass remarks from!” he shouted across the fjord to the ferryman. “You’re not even trying to be clever; you’re just using these boasts to insult me to my face!” He could have sworn he saw Graybeard grin from the other side of the fjord.

“Why, I got them from the ancient men in the woods, of course!” Graybeard said.

“You mean from the dead men hanged as common criminals in the woods?” cried Thor. “That’s some way to refer to them!”

“Well, they certainly taught me how to talk well, didn’t they?” Graybeard replied.

Thor held his hammer high and waved it, eyes burning with fiery anger. “And if you keep talking like that, you’ll be howling louder than the wolf when I get over there!” he hollered.

Graybeard laughed. “If you just want someone to pummel, then you’d better hurry on your way, Thor! I heard your wife Sif has a lover at home! He’s the one you want.”

Thor stomped his feet, his face angry and red. “Now you’re just saying any stupid insult that comes into your mouth!” he cried. “I think you’re lying!”

“I think I’m not,” replied Graybeard. “You’d catch that scoundrel quicker if you weren’t dragging your feet!”

Thor looked up at the sky and saw that the sun had moved. Graybeard was wasting his time.

"Dammit Graybeard, you bastard!" Thor roared. "You've held me up for too long! Row the boat over here and give me passage across!"

"No," Graybeard finally said. "You can walk instead."

Thor stomped his feet again and huffed some more, but it wasn't as if he could bash the man on the head from the other side of the fjord, and he couldn't throw his hammer without blowing up a mountain. All he could do was stand there, grumbling on the shore.

"Well if you refuse to offer me passage, can you at least tell me how to go the long way around?" Thor asked.

Graybeard gave Thor's request a moment's thought. "I suppose it's a small enough thing," he replied. "Go far down that path beside you until you get to the stockade, then keep walking until you reach the stone dividing the road in two. Take the fork to the left and then keep going until you come to the countryside. You will recognize it as where your mother lives, and she'll show you the way back to Asgard."

Thor glanced down the path that Graybeard had indicated.

"Will this journey take me longer than the day?" Thor probed, for the ferryman had delayed him all morning.

"Perhaps you can get there before the sun sets, if you hurry," Graybeard answered him.

And with that, Thor turned to head down the road that the ferryman had pointed to.

"Goodbye, and good riddance, Graybeard!" Thor huffed. "Next time we meet, I'll make sure my hammer gives you a proper 'thanks.'"

And as Graybeard watched Thor vanish, he threw one last insult at the thunder-god's back: "May you go where the monsters get you!"

As it stands, though, Thor never did see that ferryman again.

THOR'S DEATH IN RAGNAROK

Ragnarok means "the destiny of the gods ." This destiny was foretold by a seeress, who saw a terrible end for the Aesir. But, as it turns out, the Aesir's own careless actions created this outcome, for all their deaths came at the hands of those they disenfranchized. Thor's death, in particular, is due to the Midgard Serpent, Jormungand.

The events that led to Thor's death began early in the history of the Aesirs.

At the dawn of time, while the gods were playing in the fields without a single care in the world, Odin sought the prophecy of an old seeress. She saw the fate of the gods: a war where people forgot their kinship with one another, a time when all light left their realities, and where the sky came crashing down into the sea and all the world burned.

The seeress also saw a wolf named Fenrir escape from his bonds and swallow Odin whole. She saw all of the dead in the underworld escape to fight the gods, and a giant serpent kill Odin's son, Thor, with his venom.

This terrified the Allfather, who sought to do everything he could to prevent these events from happening.

One day, Loki brought home three beings borne of his consort, Angrboda. The first was named Fenrir, who was a wolf. The second was named Hel, who was a living girl on one side of her body and a blue corpse on the other. And the last was Jormungand, then just a small serpent who could wrap himself around Loki's shoulders. It was this serpent who would spell the eventual downfall of Odin's son, Thor.

Afraid of these creatures, Odin decided that he should immediately get rid of Loki's children. He had Fenrir bound, banished Hel to the realm of the dead, and cast Jormungand into the sea. There, the serpent grew to such a tremendous size that his whole body encircled the globe, but no one noticed this because he was sunk so deep beneath the waves.

Thor, meanwhile, learned that the best

way to vanquish an enemy was either to bash them with his hammer or threaten to bash them with his hammer. He had quite a temper, after all, and on some days the antics of his uncle, Loki, got the better of him. When Loki caused him problems, he flew into a rage and threatened him until he fixed it, and the other Aesir did the same.

Due to this poor treatment, Loki's mischief became less playful and more malicious as time went on, until he was filled with nothing but contempt for any praise the Aesir gave to other people.

Thor had a half-brother, Balder, who was as gentle as he was strong. He brought light to people's worlds and created bliss wherever he went.

When Balder began to dream of his own death, his father Odin and his mother Frigg tried to make him immune to this fate by asking all things in the world to promise never to hurt him.

Loki, however, had become so bitter by this time that he was determined to find the exception to this. Using trickery, he discovered that the mistletoe hadn't given its pledge to Frigg because she purposely hadn't asked for it, so Loki quickly crafted an arrow made from the plant. Balder was shot by this arrow, and all light left Asgard.

The Aesir's world spiraled into chaos from that moment onward. At one of Aegir's feasts, Loki insulted all the gods in attendance until they called on Thor to chase him out.

Thor's uncle then hid in the mountains, first in a house and then as a salmon in a stream. But it wasn't long before the Aesir caught him, with Thor hauling Loki out of the water by his tail. They then bound Loki deep beneath the earth.

Very soon after that, the events of Ragnarok came to pass. Jormungand, who normally held his tail in his jaws, released it, causing an earthquake so powerful that it shook all the world's bindings apart. Fenrir ran free, all Helheim broke loose, and Loki escaped his bonds to fight against the gods. All the giants joined Jormungand, Fenrir, and Loki too, tired of Thor slaughtering their kind with such impunity.

Jormungand did not forget how Thor had wounded him during a fishing trip long ago and was determined to get his revenge. Thor fought against the mighty serpent once more, his hammer booming as it crashed down on Jormungand's skull. Lightning crashed, striking the serpent, and he fell with a deafening shriek. But Thor didn't come away unscathed. One of the serpent's fangs pierced him, poisoning him. Thor took nine steps away from the creature's body before he collapsed in the rubble, dead.

And so that was the fate of the gods who orchestrated the outcomes of their own demise.

CHAPTER 4:

THOR IN THE WORLD

As one of the most widely worshipped and well-known Norse gods, Thor has existed in various incarnations throughout the ages, never truly fading from people's minds. The fact that he's always been a storm-god is certain, but in what capacity he serves and the superstitions surrounding Thor have changed over time.

THOR BEFORE AND DURING THE VIKING AGE

Odin was the favorite of poets, being emblematic of kingship and poetry, but Thor was perhaps the most worshipped Norse god due to sheer numbers alone. As the god of the common people, he was the most popular and his cult was widespread.

We know of Thor's popularity and prevalence due to the number of archaeological finds and place names associated with him. Unfortunately, the pagan Norse people never wrote anything down concerning their religion in any long format, so we have no firsthand written accounts about the specifics of Thor worship. Knowledge of the Norse gods and their mythology was transferred via the oral traditions, and while these still exist, they have changed through the centuries with a gradual loss of information. It was only later, after the conversion to Christianity, that written accounts began to appear.

THOR'S NAME IN THE WORLD

Many places in the Nordic countries are named after deities. These are place names or toponyms, and their presence shows that a god was worshipped in that region. The more frequent and widespread a god's name, the broader was his worship.

Thor's name appears in many place names across Scandinavia. Some examples include the mountain ridge Thórsmörk in Iceland, Torshälla and Torsklint in Sweden, Tórshavn (Thor's Harbor), the capital of the Faroe Islands, and various places called Þórshof in Norway. Some references to Thor potentially exist as far as Germany, England, and Ireland!

Places weren't the only things named after Thor. People also incorporated Thor into first names. Indeed, we've found names such as Torbjörn, Torsten, Torgerd, Torkel, Torun, and more written on Viking Age runestones, while other names, like Thorstein and Thorgill, also reflect Thor's name. But it would seem that places and people were rarely named simply "Thor"—evidently, this was reserved for the god alone.

ARCHAEOLOGICAL FINDS

A number of Viking Age runestones depict Thor and his hammer, and many more Norse artifacts reference him in some way, from small statues to carvings and even jewelry. These finds include mjolnir pendants, which look like small hammers. Legend has it that Thor was able to shrink his hammer to such a small size that he could wear it around his neck... though whether this legend was invented before or after these pendants became popular remains a mystery.

Mjolnir pendants were typically made of metals such as lead, iron, or silver, but others made out of amber and even sandstone have also been discovered. Wooden pendants might have existed but have been lost to time and decay.

Many of these mjolnirs were simple in design, but others were very elaborate and even made of rich materials such as gold. Although Thor is associated with common people, the wealthy may also have held him dear.

TACITUS'S GERMANIA

While we don't have firsthand accounts of Norse worship, we do have second- and third-hand ones written in pre-Christian times. One of these accounts is *Germania*, an ethnography of the Germanic peoples that was written by the Roman politician Publius Cornelius Tacitus in 98 BCE.

Germania is not especially reliable as an account of Norse worship, but is more an example of Roman nationalist propaganda than an ethnography. What's more, Tacitus never actually visited the Germanic peoples, sourcing all his information from libraries and interviews instead. Nevertheless, he does mention the Norse gods in *Germania*, noting that the Germanic people primarily worshipped Mercury (Woden/Odin), Hercules (Thor), Mars (Tyr), and Isis (an unknown goddess). The fact that Thor features in this text shows he was worshipped as far back as 98 BCE, and was prominent enough to be mentioned by a writer living in a distant country.

THOR IN MEDIEVAL TIMES

Most history books mark the beginning of the Scandinavian medieval times, and end of the Viking Age, with the Battle of Stamford Bridge, which took place between the English army and Norwegian invaders in 1066 CE.

The name of the battle is derived from a single unidentified bridge that served as a bottleneck for the English army, and a single unnamed Viking who mounted a defense on the bridge. This Viking warrior cut down as many as 40 English soldiers before meeting his own demise, after which the Norwegians were slaughtered. The English army were defeated three weeks later. Allegorically this event marks a decline in Viking activities and the coming to an end of Norse civilization. Through a combination of Christianization, political changes, shifting borders, and simply moving around a lot, the Norse people's society was so transformed that it had become something other than Norse by that point. Yet every Scandinavian I have spoken to refers to the Norse people as their ancestors and the Viking Age as their immediate history. The fact that this is a pagan history doesn't diminish its importance in any way.

This history was even acknowledged by medieval Icelandic writers, who, despite being Christian, took it upon themselves to write down the cultural stories (mythology) of the Norse gods. These are mostly found in the *Poetic* and *Prose Eddas*. The existence of these texts and others has given us a significant amount of Thor-related content, and preserves stories that were becoming endangered in the oral traditions.

THOR IN MEDIEVAL TEXTS AND SAGAS

We can't completely trust second- and third-hand historical accounts of paganism, and to what degree we can really depends on what the author was trying to accomplish to begin with.

Tacitus's *Germania* portrayed Germanic Paganism in ways that made Roman culture look superior. Medieval Christian writers often portrayed paganism in ways that made Christianity look like the better choice. Snorri Sturluson's *Prose Edda* is an interesting case because he wrote it to appeal to the Norwegian King Hakon's sense of shared heritage with Iceland in an attempt to bring him round to the idea of uniting under Icelandic rule.

None of these written accounts offer an unbiased picture of Norse Paganism, but rather a narrative about it. Even Snorri, who likely recounted the stories exactly as he heard them, wrapped his writings in a claim that the Aesir gods were descended from Troy. This was probably done to bypass the taboo of talking about the Norse gods as gods during a post-Christianized era.

Thor Mentioned by Adam of Bremen

Adam of Bremen was a medieval chronicler who wrote *Gesta Hammaburgensis ecclesiae pontificum* (Latin for "Deeds of the Bishops of Hamburg") sometime between 1073 and 1076. This book recounts activities of the

Hamburg-Bremen diocese, and because the Christian conversion of Scandinavia was well underway during Adam's time, it makes references to Norse religions.

One of the most famous passages within this text describes a certain temple at Gamla Uppsala in Sweden. Adam claims the temple was decked with gold, with a grove beside it and a tree that was evergreen throughout the year. Within the temple were statues of three gods: Odin, Thor, and Fricco (Frey). Thor was positioned in the middle of the other two, "being the mightiest" of these gods, and described as a god who presided over the air, thus governing "the thunder and lightning, the winds and rains, fair weather [and] crops."

While there was indeed a temple at Gamla Uppsala, we don't know for sure whether it was pagan. It's possible this temple was actually a Christian church that Adam of Bremen characterized as pagan in order to slander it for not cooperating with the Holy Roman Empire. He made a point of describing rather gratuitous animal and human sacrifices and also expressed disgust at the songs and processions practiced there.

But despite describing the temple and its activities in fearful ways, it's clear that Adam was familiar with the Norse pantheon. The way in which he portrays Thor, Odin, and Frey is, in fact, an accurate description of how they were seen, associating Thor with storms, Odin with battle-fury, and Frey with fertility.

Thor's prominent position between Odin and Frey may have been a result of his popularity, or was perhaps due to Adam's comparison of Thor to the god Jupiter, head of the Roman pantheon. Either way, this tells us that Thor was still a significant god even a thousand years after *Germania* was written.

Thor in the Poetic Edda

The *Poetic Edda* preserves the cultural stories and poetry that existed within the Scandinavian oral tradition at the time it was written, which makes it a reliable point of reference for some Norse mythology. Thor appears very prominently in this work, playing a key role in many of the poems. He appears as a main character in the following poems:

Völuspá: A seeress predicts the fate of the gods (Ragnarok), and foretells Thor's death at the hands of Jormungand (see pages 84–85).

Hárbarðsljóð: Thor and a ferryman named Graybeard (who is Odin in disguise) engage in a battle of wits (see pages 80–83)

Hymiskviða: The Aesir demand that the sea-giant Aegir host parties for them regularly. Aegir says he would if he had a cauldron big enough to brew ale for them all. So Thor and Tyr visit Tyr's relatives to fetch such a cauldron, and Thor fishes Jormungand up from the sea during the visit. This story is a patchwork of much smaller stories (see pages 70–73).

Lokasenna: Thor is called upon at the very end of this poem to stop an angry and disenfranchised Loki from slandering the Aesir at one of Aegir's parties (see illustration on the opposite page).

Þrymskviða: The giant Thrym steals Thor's hammer, and Thor disguises himself as Freyja to get it back (see pages 54–57).

Alvíssmál: A dwarf brags that he is engaged to Thor's daughter, a match that Thor disapproves of. He keeps the dwarf

talking until daybreak, and the dwarf then turns to stone in the sunlight (see pages 74–75).

Thor in the Prose Edda

The popularity that Thor enjoys in the *Poetic Edda* is also reflected in Snorri's *Prose Edda*. He appears in all four parts of the book. As well as expanding on many of the *Poetic Edda's* stories of Thor, Snorri also adds a few more, including Thor's visit to Utgard-Loki (see pages 62–69) and his battle with the giant Hrungnir (see pages 76–79).

For the most part, the myths Snorri recounts portray Thor exactly the way he's known throughout the rest of Norse mythology and the oral tradition—as a thunder-god and Odin's son. The one exception is found in the Prologue of the Prose Edda. Here Snorri explains that the gods aren't really gods but rather human ancestors. Here, Thor is the son of a Turkish king and was raised in Thrace by a duke named Loricus. Thor was handsome to look at, with hair "more beautiful than gold." He inherited his father's weapons at the age of 10 and reached his full strength at the age of 12, being capable of lifting 10 bearskins off the ground at once. After this, Thor killed his foster-father to take Thrace ("which we call Thrudheim," says Snorri), before traveling north and meeting the prophetess Sybil (Sif), who he married. Together the two of them had a son, who had a son, who had a son, and so forth, until that son had a son named Odin, who became head of the Aesir (Snorri explains that the Aesir are called this because they're from Asia).

We must consider that Snorri was writing in a Christian environment, and during his time it was taboo to speak favorably about pagan gods or record their myths. Snorri may have added this Prologue as a way of working around this taboo; he could claim that his work wasn't about pagan gods, but our

ancestors instead. Though who knows why he made the history so absurd? He doesn't confuse Thor and Odin's lineages at any other point and doesn't expand upon this history any further.

Thor in Heimskringla

Heimskringla is a medieval saga of disputed authorship, but some scholars attribute it to Snorri. It is a historical account of Swedish and Norwegian kings. Similar to other medieval histories, it starts with a mythologized past and gradually becomes more reliable in its historicity as it continues.

The first part of this work is called the *Ynglinga* saga, which deals with the mythologized past, more specifically the saga of the Ynglings, a legendary Swedish dynasty. Thor is mentioned here, once again portrayed as a human, but this time he's described as a gothi (a pagan priest-chief) to whom Odin gave Thrudheim. This book also provides a record of the names attributed to Thor.

THOR IN MEDIEVAL FOLKLORE

Thor-related folklore endured despite the decline of paganism, finding its way into legends, superstitions, and even folk magic. Much like the Norse oral traditions, this folklore varies from region to region.

Tales of St. Olaf

The arrival of Christianity in Norway had a great impact on its culture and folklore due to the aggressive nature of Norway's conversion. Norwegian kings—including a certain Olaf Haraldsson, who later became St. Olaf or Olaf the Holy—used Christianity as a device for gaining power and control during the Viking Age.

The historical figure of Olaf Haraldsson is very different to the saint he became. He was born in 995 CE to Harald Grenske, a petty Norwegian king in Vestfold, and baptized at the age of three by his godfather, Olaf Tryggvason. The young Olaf Haraldsson went on many Viking campaigns, during which he acquired great skills as a warrior. Eventually, he returned to his homelands and seized the throne, striving to convert the region to Christianity during his 15-year reign. However, his violent and aggressive tactics made him unpopular among his subjects, to the point that they either killed him or chased him out (sources contemporary to Olaf report different fates for this Viking king).

Yet the story of Olaf Haraldsson's sainthood depicts him as dying in the Battle of Stiklestad in 1030 CE. Olaf was canonized a year after his death and became an instrumental figure in converting the Vikings to Christianity.

The story of St. Olaf is linked to the Norse god Thor because he took on Thor's characteristics, possessing a flaming red beard and a battle-ax for eradicating trolls and other baneful spirits. St. Olaf is associated with fertility and protection, just like Thor, and is also depicted as quick to anger.

In nearly all ways, St. Olaf stepped into the role that Thor once fulfilled for the Norse people, becoming a Christian spirit who protected them against malignant pagan beings.

Swedish Folklore

While Thor was replaced by the image of St. Olaf in Norway, Swedish folklore still mentions Thor in various places. Some of these superstitions potentially date back as far as medieval times.

A Hammer Is Used to Promise Boys

There are places in Sweden that had a custom of placing a hammer or sledgehammer under a newly married couple's bed on their wedding night, to ensure their first child would be a boy. The folklorist Ebbe Shön recounts a particularly humorous tale from Gotland, in which some friends of the groom placed an oversized sledgehammer under the bed, resulting in the couple having two sons and no daughter. This is reminiscent of an event in the story of the theft of Thor's hammer (see pages 54–57), during which the giant Thrym places a hammer on "Freya's" lap to bless the bride.

Lucky Finds

Legends of Thor's indestructible hammer aren't always found in the oral traditions, however. Instead, some farming communities in rural Sweden believed Thor had to use a different weapon every time. While working, farmers would sometimes dig up interesting objects such as stone axes, fire-starting rocks, or even just nature-created stones with strange and unique shapes. While many of these were neolithic objects, the farmers believed a tale that these objects were weapons thrown by the god Thor while he was hunting trolls and other nasty spirits, and were therefore extremely powerful for warding off evil. They would hang these objects above the doors of their storehouse to ward off malicious spirits, in the same way that they would paint crosses on their buildings to provide protection. (It was common practice to invoke the protections of both Christian and Norse figures in post-Christianized Scandinavia.)

Superstitions about Lightning

A Swedish superstition around lightning has it that you should never have your clothes unbuttoned or your skirts tied up during a thunderstorm, so that trolls don't try to hide in the folds. That way, Thor won't be tempted to strike you with lightning in his efforts to slay them.

Likewise, it is considered unsafe to stand under trees during a thunderstorm, because that might put you in the way of trolls trying to seek refuge under their branches, and therefore bring Thor's lightning down on your head. (In the post Viking Age, trolls have taken the place of giants, reflecting a belief that Thor had killed off all the giants or that they had disappeared long ago.)

Roll on the Ground for Good Health

The Swedish scholar and diplomat Gunnar Olof Hyltén-Cavallius wrote sometime in the 1860s about a ritual

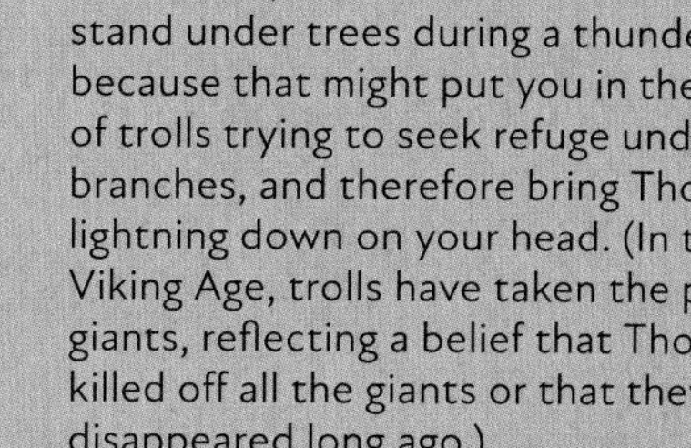

from Värend that goes something like this: When you first hear Thor driving his chariot in the spring, roll on the ground to prevent backaches and hit your head with a stone to prevent headaches. The latter may be a reference to the whetstone that was lodged in Thor's head during his fight with Hrungnir, which causes him headaches (see pages 76–79).

A similar belief exists in Jämtland and Hälsingland, where it's thought that rolling on the ground during thunderstorms promises a good harvest.

Thor Lives in Many Places

Place names typically have legends attached to them that explain the name. Thor has quite a few of these in Sweden, such as Torshall in Västergötland and Torsklint in Östergötland—these are places he was thought to live.

There is also an ancient hillfort on the Swedish island of Gotland called Torsburgen (meaning "Thor's fort"), and, as the name suggests, this fort is tied to many different legends of Thor. One such legend has it that Thor's gravesite is located here. This legend probably isn't literal, since no tomb has been found on Torsburgen, but it may be a metaphor for the eventual demise of the fort: The state of the ruins suggests invading enemies burned down Torsburgen's walls and likely destroyed the interior. This may have been seen as an act of "killing Thor"—that is, killing that which protected and defended people.

Thor is also associated with various wellsprings across Scandinavia. A few of them include a wellspring in Gotland known as Thor's well, one in Södertälje called *Thores Källa* ("the well of Thore"), and one called *Helga Thors Källa* ("well of the sacred Thor") in Småland.

Thor... Friend of the Giants?

Later folklore sometimes depicts Thor as a friend of giants rather than their enemy, which potentially came from the notion that Thor and giants are of the same pagan ilk compared to Christian figures. One example of this can be found in a folk song from the parish of Naverstad in northern Bohuslän, which tells a tale of a mountain-giant calling his animals home from grazing and evoking his powerful friend Thor in the process.

Thor in Scandinavian Folk Magic

Thor's function as a protector-figure remained in the popular imagination throughout the Middle Ages, even arising in Scandinavian magical practices. Among the Icelandic grimoires—books of spells—is a work called the *Huld* manuscript (or "dark" manuscript), which was compiled by Geir Vigfússon in 1847. This grimoire contains information about Icelandic magical staves, including one called *Þórshamar*, which can be used by magicians to expose thieves.

Thor is also sometimes mentioned and evoked in the Scandinavian folk practice called trolldom. For example, one spell from the 18th century describes a troll-formula for taking water from one of Thor's various sacred wells.

THOR'S EARLY MODERN-DAY REPRESENTATIONS

Though the Norse gods survived in Scandinavian folklore, they only began to reach a global audience from around the 1800s, with the rise of German Romanticism and the creation of the European Studies field.

German Romanticism was a cultural movement that began around the mid- to late 19th century in Germany. It was marked by a growing interest in uncovering Germany's pre-Christian past. As a nation fraught by a history of ever-changing borders and power struggles, the German people longed to find stability in a shared cultural identity, and began to look to history for the answers.

Among these thinkers were the famous duo Jacob and Wilhelm Grimm, better known as the Brothers Grimm. While best known for writing and compiling collections of German fairy tales, they were also interested in reconstructing the ancient culture and beliefs of pagan Germany.

The only problem was that this was a very new field of study, and being pioneers in the field, the Grimm brothers' reconstruction methods were very flawed. They saw similarities between the German languages and the Scandinavian ones, and made an error of assuming that these linguistic similarities indicated shared cultural correlations. And so, they and other thinkers began to look to the Nordic past as a way of filling in the gaps of the Germanic one… and still through a romanticizing lens.

This reached its peak with Richard Wagner's epic four-part opera, *Der Ring des Nibelungen*, which was first performed in part in the year 1869. This opera featured one of the very first pop-cultural representations of the Norse deities within modern times. While its other movements are about legendary heroes, its first movement, called *Das Rheingold*, features the Norse gods.

Thor appears in this opera as his German cognate, Donner. He's portrayed as the hot-tempered god of thunder and the brother of Wotan's (Odin's) wife, Fricka (Frigg). But unlike his characterization within the Norse myths, Thor's role in *Das Rheingold* is rather minor. Nevertheless, this portrayal inspired a new slew of art depicting the Norse gods, and likewise paved the way for Thor's modern-day representations.

THOR TODAY

Thor has never been a complicated figure compared to some of the other Norse gods. His modern-day worship looks very similar to his historical worship; he's still called upon for protection, still the defender of mankind, and still associated with thunderstorms.

The main difference is that Thor is now worshipped in locations beyond Scandinavia as well as places within it, and acknowledged by Heathens across the globe. Worship of Thor has steadily grown in the United States with the rise of Norse Paganism and of using Thor hammer pendants to indicate veneration of the Norse gods (and especially Thor).

THOR IN POP CULTURE

Perhaps due to how conducive Thor's character is to the modern-day superhero genre, he's appeared (and continues to appear) in a plethora of different movies, comics, games, and other media. Most of Thor's depictions take liberties with his portrayal and capabilities, so, while seeing him in modern-day media is entertaining, keep in mind that some of the portrayals are character adaptations of Thor, rather than depictions of the god himself.

Thor in Comics

Thor has appeared in comics almost since their conception. Some of the most well-known include the Danish *Valhalla* comics, which began in 1979. These feature Thor, Loki, and Odin as main characters. Other comics include Marvel's *Thor* comics, which depict Thor as a superhero, and Neil Gaiman's *Sandman* series.

Thor in Movies and on TV

Thor has made his way into many movies, shows, and animations. Perhaps the most well-known of these is Thor's appearance in the Marvel Cinematic Universe. Though Thor is still depicted as the son of Odin and the god of thunder, there are quite a lot of differences in family dynamics, appearances, and storylines. In the myths, Thor's archenemy, for example, is actually his "uncle" Loki's child, Jormungand, the World Serpent, rather than Loki himself. Thor does not fly with the aid of his hammer, as suggested in the movies, and instead travels the sky in a chariot pulled by two goats. In the MCU, there's also a requirement for worthiness for Thor to wield his hammer—similar to Excalibur from Arthurian legend. However, Norse mythology implies that anyone with enough strength could lift it and even steal Mjolnir (see pages 54–57).

Thor in Video Games

After the success of the video game *Skyrim*, which uses Viking-esque aesthetics, the Norse gods have appeared more and more in video games. For example, Thor's hammer is featured in *Assassin's Creed: Valhalla*, and Thor himself appears as an antagonist in *God of War Ragnarok*.

CHAPTER 5:

VENERATING THOR

This section provides options and avenues for venerating Thor. Nothing here is required by any means; these are simply different approaches that Heathens take when venerating, worshipping, or otherwise working with this figure.

HOW TO VENERATE THOR

The approach taken in this guide to venerating Thor is in the vein of devotional polytheism, which focuses on the development of an interpersonal working relationship with a deity without the involvement of any mediator or doctrine. Faith—the concept of believing in something without evidence—is also not required. I offer this approach because devotional polytheism can be tailored to your existing personal philosophies regarding the nature of divinity, which makes it suitable for anyone, no matter what their current perspective is.

That being said, to better grasp how Norse deities like Thor function, it is helpful to understand something of the background from which the Old Norse religions grew.

As a decentralized worldview, the Norse outlook is said to have been animistic in nature. While animism is typically defined as "everything having a soul," this definition is based on how animism looks within the framework of Christianity, rather than outside it.

Within the context of Norse Paganism, animism can be defined as the acknowledgment of the interconnected nature of all things, and the view that all things, material and immaterial, operate as an ecosystem. The divine and the mundane are not considered separate from one another, nor opposites of each other. Because of this, the concept of "sin" doesn't apply here either—there is no action, thought, or moral circumstance that draws a person closer or farther away from a deity such as Thor. Similarly, there is no set of morals or values that one must hold to worship Thor, although some people choose to see him as a role model.

The gods are characterized as being human, but as if their humanity has taken on epic proportions. This also means that they're not perfect. They have distinct personalities, opinions, and outlooks that we may or may not always agree with, and which may or may not always sit right with us. When adopting a veneration practice with Thor, think of it as establishing a new interpersonal relationship with him, complete with the interval of "getting to know someone." What the relationship between you and Thor looks like, however, is entirely up to you and Thor.

BUILDING AN ALTAR

Popular among Norse Heathens globally is the act of building an altar or dedicated shrine to a deity. An altar is just as much for you as it is for the deity—a communal space for both of you—and being a part of your living space, it should be something you are happy with.

Some pagans make a distinction between an altar and a shrine; in which case an altar is a space for any kind of crafting or spellwork, whereas a shrine operates as more of a dedicated spot for a deity, ancestor, spirit, or multiple powers. Other pagans do not differentiate between the two, and may use the term "altar" to describe a shrine or a multipurpose space that serves both functions. For the sake of this section, I will use "altar" in the multipurpose sense.

Altars generally operate as a space where offerings are given to powers, and are decorated in ways reminiscent of those powers. They may also house the tools that people use in their practice. Altars can be big or small, simple or complex. They can be placed anywhere, for example on a windowsill or bookshelf, in a shoebox, on a table, on a floating shelf, or even in a virtual space. I have heard of people building temples for their deities in Minecraft servers, or creating websites that serve as digital shrines. Other clever ways to create altars include scrapbooking or creating a shadow-box similar to a diorama. In this way, altars can be overt or covert, and tailored to your space and needs.

Some people like to take a very historical approach to altars and place them outdoors. Groves were thought to be sacred spaces in the ancient past, so anyone with a backyard or outside space may take the opportunity to build one out there.

How an altar is decorated is up to the individual. Most people have a spot on the altar where they can give offerings. Altars may also feature some form of iconography of the deity, whether in the form of two-dimensional art or a three-dimensional sculpture. Decorative features, such as candles, lights, garlands, altar cloths, or stones, may also be added.

Some altars are thematic and play hard into the Viking theme, with animal pelts and drinking horns, while others are more contemporary in appearance. Others are themed according to the personality of the deity to whom they are dedicated.

An altar should bring you joy in its function as a devotional space. If approaching your altar creates a feeling of apprehension or spiritual obligation within you, then you could try rearranging it to be more personable, or even test out a different format.

BLÓT, OR OFFERINGS

Blót **(pronounced "bloat") means "offering" or "blessing," and describes the giving of a gift. The act of making offerings to a deity is referred to as performing *blót*.**

Sometimes, *blót* has been mistranslated as meaning "blood," in the sense of offering a blood sacrifice, but this is a false etymology. Similarly, the translation of the word as "sacrifice" somewhat misrepresents what *blót* is all about. While an offering is a sacrifice in the sense that it is something that's given, the term "sacrifice" suggests trial or difficulty; that the harder it is to give something up, the more valuable it is as an offering.

That being said, Thor is a very casual god and doesn't necessarily need much extravagance when it comes to offerings, although he does appreciate it when people go the extra mile to offer something special. However, this image of "sacrifice" runs contrary to a lot of Scandinavian cultural concepts around reciprocity. In truth, the Norse gods would not want us to perform acts in their name that are detrimental to our own wellbeing.

Instead, the way in which an offering is typically given in Heathenry is in the spirit of *frith*. This word is often crudely translated as meaning "peace," but it more accurately describes the state that emerges from mutually enjoyed companionship. Giving gifts in *frith* is the act of giving from a place of human connection, which means it should be an enjoyable experience for all involved.

HOW TO MAKE AN OFFERING

There are a few general steps to follow when making an offering, which will ensure you evoke the correct deity, and not an impostor, and offer something they would appreciate.

There are many different ways to give an offering to Thor. Some people make offerings in a formal manner, while others do so more casually. Some people make offerings on a routine basis, while others make them whenever the mood strikes. It really all boils down to what you prefer.

However, it's usually common courtesy to give offerings when you are asking for favors from Thor, as well as after that favor has been fulfilled. It's also good manners to offer something when you're first introducing yourself to him. Holiday offerings are also popular, particularly when there's already ample food that can be shared, or when it's a holiday with which Thor is especially associated.

Here are the four steps for making an offering to Thor.

1

DECIDE WHAT IT IS YOU WANT TO OFFER

Usual offerings consist of food and/or drink, but offerings of trinkets, artwork, poetry, songs, scents, and other gifts also count (for a list of suggestions, see pages 108–110). What you offer doesn't have to be elaborate or "traditional." It's more important that it's heartfelt and genuine. Half a candy bar can be just as meaningful as a fancy home-cooked meal if it is given in the spirit of friendship.

You also don't have to offer a great deal of whatever it is. Thor doesn't necessarily need to eat the same quantities we do. I offer what generally fits into an average dipping-sauce bowl, and also have a small drinking horn on a stand for libations. Some Heathens have dedicated crockery and cutlery for offerings, while others simply use what they have available in their home kitchen.

2

CLEANSE, BLESS, AND CONSECRATE YOUR OFFERING MATERIALS

This is something that will make the offering more appetizing. Not only do you want to make sure that your offering materials are clean, you also need to be certain they are cleansed.

Cleansing can be thought of as prepping the energy of the material in the same way that cleaning preps the body of the material. Cleansing can be as simple as running the dishes you're about to use under water and soap, and imbuing them with the energies of cleanliness. To do this, put the sensation of "cleanliness" in your hands and into the act of cleaning the dishes. This is what some people characterize as putting an intention into the act.

For any utensils that can't have prolonged exposure to water and dish soap for any reason, the usual method of cleaning and prepping them works just as well. For example, silver can be cleansed during the polishing process, cast iron can be cleansed during the seasoning process, and steel blades can be cleansed during oiling. Simply taking a soft cloth to "wipe away" residual energy can also be effective for cleansing.

During the cleansing process, you may want to bless and consecrate the material. A blessing puts good tidings into it, while consecrating it is the act of giving it its function. For example, if you are preparing a drinking horn to use as an offering vessel, you can say something like:

"May this offering horn have a long and cared-for existence in its function as an offering vessel for the gods."

Speech is considered a powerful vehicle for imbuing intention into something within Norse practices. Language, however, is actually optional in this respect. Something can be spoken through the medium of feelings and actions, so long as you're actually communicating to the object rather than merely visualizing your intention in your mind.

The food and/or beverage may also be blessed, if you wish.

3

EVOKE THOR

Once your offering is prepared, it's time to call Thor to the space. This can be as simple as approaching your altar and saying a few words. Personally, I like to light candles to draw attention to the altar and set the tone for the space.

If you are evoking Thor for the first time, it's important to really think about the reason. Some people approach Thor simply for friendship or for wisdom and advice. Some are looking for a connection to the past, while others do so because they are looking for a father figure.

There's nothing we can approach the gods about that they haven't dealt with before. Even if you don't know what it is you're looking for, just be honest about it. Thor doesn't mind wanderers and may even be able to give you some pointers.

What you say when you give the offering and how you say it are entirely up to you, although it's good to be honest, courteous, and polite. Make it clear that you are evoking Thor and nobody else.

4

GIVE THE OFFERING

There are many ways that offerings can be transported to the deity. For food/drink offerings, you can leave the offering out for a while before disposing of it or consuming it (perhaps on behalf of Thor). If you are outdoors, you can give the offering to the earth or throw it into a burning firepit. It's sensible not to leave food offerings out for so long that they spoil or attract pests. If you struggle to clean up food offerings for one reason or another, consider using non-perishable offerings. If all else fails, water is always a welcome universal offering for any situation.

Non-food offerings such as artwork can be presented or left at the altar. If you're dedicating a song, then make sure to evoke the deity that you've dedicated it to before performing.

THOR'S FAVORITE OFFERINGS

Like people, deities always enjoy receiving presents. And, like people, they are especially partial to particular presents. While Thor enjoys receiving all kinds of gifts—and I invite you to explore what they are—there are a few items that he's known to be fond of within the oral traditions.

FOOD

The Norse myths characterize Thor as a big eater who easily puts away any food set before him... and then some! Thor's favorite foods have not changed all that much throughout the ages, and tend to be the same as those he's often depicted eating within the myths. These were the foods also typically offered to him in ancient times.

Meats

Thor is a big fan of meats, from the humble grilled chicken to the magnificent pulled pork. He enjoys steak, hams, and fish of all kinds. Bacon is also a big hit, and he even enjoys our newer processed meats such as hot dogs, bratwurst, and salami. He is very fond of hamburgers too, especially if they're loaded.

Bread and Grains

Since grains and cereals were an important source of nutrition among the farmers of Scandinavia, any grain-based products are very appropriate to offer to Thor, especially since his wife, Sif, is associated with wheat. For this reason, Thor is pleased with any offerings of bread, oatmeal, and similar products. Homemade bread in particular makes for a loving gift.

Cheeses

In addition to enjoying meat, Thor also likes animal products such as cheeses. Goat cheese is an especially good offering for Thor, due to his association with goats.

Echoing Thor's association with meats and grains, platter foods such as cheese, meat, and crackers are excellent offerings.

Hearty Foods

As a god who is always busy and on the go, Thor's preferred foods tend to be anything that is hearty and sustaining. Soups, stews, and chilis make wonderful offerings to Thor, as well as any hearty breakfasts. The all-American breakfast of eggs, hash browns, and bacon (or some other meat like sausage) is great to share with Thor, as well as portions of feast-like meals, such as foods prepared for holidays or similarly special occasions.

Cakes and Sweets

Although Thor enjoys hearty foods, he will never say no to dessert. He enjoys cakes, cookies, pies, milkshakes, and other such treats. These do not necessarily have to be homemade in order to be welcomed and appreciated!

BEVERAGES

Libations have long been given to gods as offerings. Thor is a fan of many different beverages, but below are a few of his favorites.

Mead

Thor loves mead and is always happy to receive it! The myths often depict him drinking mead by the barrelful whenever he's at gatherings. Mead is also the most traditional alcoholic offering that can be given to any of the Norse gods, not just to Thor.

Mead is also known as honey wine due to the fact it's distilled from honey. Because of the nature of honey, mead can have an extremely wide profile of flavors, ranging from super sweet to dry, to spicy, to fruity. Thor will happily take any mead you pick out for him.

Beer and Ale

While mead was considered a special beverage in ancient times, beer and ale were perhaps the most common. These beverages will also be a good go-to drink to offer Thor, particularly if mead is harder to come by. And no, these drinks don't need to be fancy either!

Mulled Wine

Mulled wine, also known as *glögg* in Sweden, is a kind of spiced red wine brewed during the winter holidays. While recipes vary, it's typically comprised of a red wine mixed with spices such as ginger, cloves, cardamom pods, cinnamon sticks, orange peel, a sweetener, and another alcohol such as brandy, aquavit, or vodka. This brew is great for creating the toasty-warm feelings of *hygge* during the cold winter months, and is another great option to give to Thor.

Milk

Thor is Odin's son and a warrior at heart, and associated to a degree with the warrior class known as *Berserkers*, or "bear-skins." These warriors got their prowess and fearlessness in battle by assuming a wild, animal-like state of mind, which they activated by consuming certain psychoactive substances. Due to the nature of these substances, they would first have to distill out the toxins. This was accomplished by feeding the substances to cows and then consuming the animal by-product, such as the milk. Milk therefore makes a great offering to Thor in honor of this memory.

Water

If all else fails, water is a welcome offering for Thor. While seemingly mundane in comparison to mead or ale, water is actually one of the best universal offerings, and the act of sharing water is one of the oldest gestures of *frith*, or peace, that we have. Thor appreciates water at any time.

ART AND ACTIVITIES

In addition to food offerings, typical offerings to Norse gods include feats of artistry, skill, and craftsmanship. These don't always have to be the most skilled of creations, and it's more important that they come from a place of genuine feeling. Here are some things often dedicated to Thor.

Workouts

It's not uncommon for those who venerate Thor to devote exercise or strength-training to him. Workouts are dedicated to Thor to honor his association with strength and to show appreciation for him and his qualities. In a way this is also used to bless the workout, and to have Thor watch over it and see that it goes well. Thor's hall is said to be "strength," and this is the act of experiencing strength itself rather than a physical location. This makes places such as gyms close to Thor's hall, and therefore close to Thor.

Poetry

In ancient times, kings, warriors, and heroes would hire poets to compose poems about their deeds. Composing devotional poetry for Thor makes for a great offering for him and is a wonderful way to honor him.

The poetry doesn't need to have a set format. While the skalds of ancient times would use complex poetic formats, people today craft their poetry in a freeform style or in other formats that suit their skills, intentions, and language. Thor appreciates any approach to singing his praises, whatever form it takes!

THOR'S SPECIAL DAYS

Although we don't have detailed records of all the Norse holidays—which varied across time and place—there are a few days associated with Thor in modern-day Heathenry.

THURSDAY

All the English names for the days of the week, with the exception of Saturday, are named after the Norse gods. Thursday means "Thor's day," which makes this a perfect day for venerating Thor.

Plenty of superstitions circulate in Swedish folklore about Thursday, as recounted by folklorist Ebbe Shön. For example, Thursday nights were held as sacred, and during them it was important to keep silent and to avoid circular motions of any sort. There is no explanation as to why, however.

Folklore from 1860s' Värend mentions that Thor and his wife may come to visit on Thursday evenings, which is why the house must be kept swept.

Thursday evenings were also often times to hold feasts. While this may be because of the Christian custom of fasting on Fridays, it might also be a remnant of pre-Christian beliefs surrounding Thursdays.

Lastly, Thursdays were also thought to be a day when supernatural forces were easiest to contact, which may or may not have some connection to Thor.

ÞORRABLÓT

Þorrablót (pronounced "Thorrablot") is a historical Icelandic holiday associated with the god Þorri, a figure who personifies winter. *Þorrablót* was celebrated on the first day of Þorri, the name of a month from the old Icelandic calendar that correlates with mid-January to mid-February.

However, due to the Thor-sounding part of *Þorrablót*, this historical holiday is sometimes celebrated in honor of the god Thor, and toasts are made in his name around mid-January.

COMMUNICATING WITH THOR

Some people are content with worshipping a deity without any additional interaction outside of this. Others may want to experience a greater degree of socialization with a deity.

This section will go over the general basics of spirit and deity work, and give you different methods and tools that may help you in that journey.

SOME THINGS TO CONSIDER

It's very easy to get caught up in the glamor of deity work due to its "mystical" and "supernatural" nature. But these relationships work in very much the same way that mundane ones do:

You Will Still Need to Get to Know Thor

I've watched many of my fellow pagans get caught off-guard because they confused knowing a lot about Thor with having personal familiarity. No matter how much you know through research, please be prepared to learn more through your interactions.

Relationship Dynamics Matter

What's healthy in mundane interpersonal relationships is also healthy in spiritual ones, and what's unhealthy in mundane interpersonal relationships is equally unhealthy in spiritual ones.

Incompatibility Happens

Sometimes a deity's personality, methods, and antics might not vibe well with you. That's okay. Recognize when it happens and make adjustments accordingly. This may mean taking a break, putting some emotional distance between the two of you, or going your separate ways altogether.

Deity Work Takes Effort

Along with everything that comes with maintaining any relationship, deity work involves researching, learning new tools of communication, learning new skills, and accepting that there will be a process of trial and error.

This Relationship Is Between You and the Deity

No one should act as a dedicated "interpreter" between you and Thor. Avoid relying on someone else to validate your perceptions, otherwise it'll be harder for you to learn ways to validate your own.

You Can Say "No"

Just because Thor may want or suggest something, it doesn't mean you have to go along with it.

Gods Can Say "No"

The gods are not wish-granting machines that we can load prayers into until a miracle pops out. Thor is going to have his own thoughts about things, and has just as much of a right to say "no" to things as we do.

Deities Are Not Mind-Readers

Deities like Thor have a better understanding of how we might be thinking and feeling than most people do, but that doesn't mean they can read our minds, let alone see a record of everything we've ever thought.

METHODS OF COMMUNICATION

Communication can happen through many modalities. The more methods of communication you use, the more methods of confirmation you are likely to experience. It's best to use many different kinds of communication, rather than to rely on just one.

SYNCHRONICITIES

Synchronicities are signs and portents that signal the presence of a deity. They can manifest as dreams or even as physical phenomena. Synchronicities can be thought of as "coincidences that seem far too convenient to be simply coincidental," and often come in multiples. They are characterized by having an air of uncanniness about them, and usually appear when you least expect them to.

It's important to keep the concept of "multiples" in mind when it comes to synchronicities. Watching a storm as it takes its course may not be a special sign in and of itself (besides being an instance of Thor passing through), but having thunder and lightning strike at auspicious times, or seeing things such as goats, depictions of Thor or his hammer, or noticing other associations pop up at unexpected times... well, these may be an indication that he is letting you know he's there. This may be especially true after you've called upon him.

Probability plays a role in this as well. If a movie or TV show comes out that features Thor as a main character, then seeing ads or posters with him are probably not going to be signs—it's the fact that the signs are unusual in some way, or seem to "move" differently from the usual rhythm of life, that make them what they are.

Synchronicities are helpful because they allow a deity to tell you who they are in ways unique to them. The delivery may be as telling as the sign itself is, and can help you clue in not only on who the deity is, but also on who they say they are.

DIVINATION

Along with its use for fortune telling, divination can also be used to facilitate communication with Thor. After evoking him, you can use a divination method such as runes, tarot, an oracle deck, cartomancy, dice divination, or similar to ask questions and receive answers.

In order to make sure that you have the right deity, you can perform a deity interview spread (see opposite). This is also a good way to make sure who you have is authentic, as opposed to an impostor spirit (see page 118). The spread was designed for tarot but can also be used with other mediums.

Divination methods with a greater degree of random chance, such as tarot or runes, are good for verification because it's a lot harder for you to subconsciously influence the results. Methods that are easier to influence, such as pendulums, aren't reliable.

Sometimes it can be difficult to work out in the moment what a reading is saying, but recording it means you can go back and check again at a later time when your mind is clear.

DEITY INTERVIEW SPREAD

1. Who are you? This card identifies the spirit, deity, or entity in question. This roughly corresponds to how the entity sees themselves.

2. What are you known for? Think of this as the entity's history or background.

3. Name one of your traits. This is a characteristic, feature, or quality that the entity has.

4. Name one of your skills. This is a skill, talent, or area of specialization that the entity has.

5. What is something you're associated with? This can be an event, a symbolic image, or a concept that is attributed to the entity.

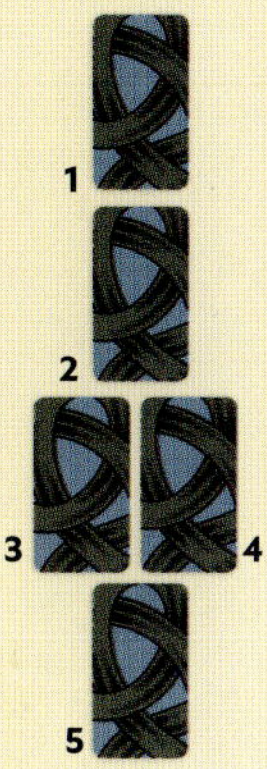

CLAIRSENSES

The clairsenses or "clear-senses" are characterized as perceptions that are roughly equivalent to our physical ones, correlating to our senses of smell, taste, hearing, touch, and sight. It's thought that clairsenses measure metaphysical stimuli rather than material ones, and therefore can be used to interact with deities in a way that's similar to interacting with anyone else.

I find this model can be misleading, because clairsenses, like "clairvoyance" (clear-seeing) or "clairsentience" (clear-thinking), are rather abstract. It also risks giving the impression that training the clairsenses is about training the physical senses to perceive metaphysical information about the world, which can actually have negative consequences.

Communicating with deities and spirits is, fortunately, a much simpler process—it's about becoming aware of what our inner senses are already detecting. I say "inner senses," because noticing what our clairsenses are doing is a byproduct of directing our awareness inward.

Establishing a connection with Thor through our clairsenses creates a direct channel of perception and communication where conversations can be exchanged in real time. That being said, how our minds experience this kind of thing is different for everyone. It's important to recognize how clairsenses manifest as sensations within yourself.

However, our ability to perceive the inner senses can be clouded by many things—our emotions, our imaginations, symptoms of mental ailments, or even an overworked nervous system. We need to use discernment at every turn and avoid taking everything at face value. Even when we are able to identify our clairsenses, discernment is still important for things such as differentiating gods from impostor spirits (see pages 116–118).

THE TOOLS OF DISCERNMENT

There are many different tools of discernment. Practicing them and strengthening them will help you to build accuracy and clarity with your spiritual perceptions.

Discernment is the act of differentiating what something is from what we think it is, as well as from what it's not. When you smell a carton of milk to check if it's spoiled, you're using discernment.

THE SANDBOX

Aristotle once famously said, "It is the mark of an educated mind to be able to entertain a thought without accepting it." This is the function of what I call the sandbox. The sandbox is a space or container in your mind where all new information goes, where you can play with it without necessarily accepting it as part of your worldview.

It allows us to consider our experiences before we decide how to interpret them. For example, if we see a raven and believe it's a sign from Thor, we need to be able to stop and ask ourselves, "Is this belief a result of the experience or a reflection of my desire for a sign?"

The sandbox is not the tool that reveals that answer for us. Rather, it's where we can "hold that thought" until we gather more information.

DISAMBIGUATION

Disambiguation is the act of telling things apart, usually by comparing and contrasting them.

Imagine you have a basket full of different kinds of apples in front of you, and you want to find the Honeycrisp. You know that a Honeycrisp has a red-yellow skin, so you easily rule out the green Granny Smith and the Red Delicious. You are left with apples that look similar, so now you use a different method to tell them apart; you might consider pattern or texture, or even start biting into them to taste-test. We can run comparisons until we have a clear idea of what it is we're looking at.

Disambiguation is something you can turn to in instances when you're not sure whether a deity is actually who they say they are, or if you're not sure whether what you're experiencing is an energy or an emotional reaction, or if you can't tell whether the dream you had was an anxiety/desire or premonition.

NOTICING

In order for us to discern things, we first need to make sure we're actually noticing them. Notice, for example, how your body is positioned. Notice yourself reading the words on these pages. With enough practice, it's possible to even notice ourselves during moments of intense anger or sadness; we "float" above our emotions and observe them even in the middle of having them.

Noticing allows us to examine the things we are perceiving, regardless of the thoughts or feelings we have in relation to them. This is important for perceiving the inner senses, because it allows us to interpret them accurately, as opposed to interpreting things the way we wish them to be.

CONFIRMATION BIAS

This is less of a discernment tool and more of a phenomenon to be aware of. Confirmation bias is defined as "the tendency to search for, interpret, favor, and recall information that confirms or supports your prior personal beliefs or values." In other words, it's the act of finding evidence to support your beliefs, rather than basing your beliefs on evidence.

It's hard not to have hopes for certain outcomes with deity and spirit work, but finding evidence to support our hopes will not guarantee their manifestation; it will only support the story we have in our minds. The more you work against confirmation bias, the more authentic your interactions with Thor will be.

ON DEITY WORK AND MENTAL ILLNESS

Some people wonder how to tell the difference between clairsenses and the manifestation of a preexisting mental ailment. The answer is that it really depends on the symptoms you experience and how your clairsenses manifest. As a general rule, though, I always recommend doing check-ins with yourself as you continue with deity work. Ask yourself:

- Is this work interfering with my day-to-day life?
- Is this causing me distress, anxiety, confusion, or disruption in any way?
- Am I having a hard time with discernment in general right now?

If your practice is giving you undue distress, then it may be good to set some boundaries with it. As intriguing as deity work is, your sense of stability in the world comes first.

MENTAL SOCK PUPPETS

A mental "sock puppet" is the result of you talking to yourself and interpreting that self-talk as an entity. Here are some signs you might be dealing with a mental sock puppet:

- It acts in accordance with your whims and expectations.
- You receive no "new" or unique information from interacting with the sock puppet.
- The sock puppet is only as knowledgeable as you are.

- It has no autonomous nature (it only abides by your will).
- It gives no portents or signs unless you're looking for them.

Mental sock puppets only exist for as long as we use them, and the way to stop using them is to draw our awareness to their existence.

IMPOSTORS

Not all entities may be what they seem, and it's possible to encounter things that disguise themselves as Thor, especially if this is your first foray into deity work. That's why it's important to check to make sure you have the entity you think you have before committing.

It's possible for petty spirits to impersonate deities for their own gain. These impostor spirits are more opportunists than actual threats.

A simple way to make sure you have the real Thor is to deliberately evoke the thunder-god when you plan to interact with him. That, and warding your space (see right). Impostors usually aren't professional actors, and can be spotted by a number of telltale behaviors. Some of these behaviors are red-flag actions, such as:

- They refuse to let you interact with other entities or people, or do further research on them.
- They claim they can give you everything you want, preying on your insecurities, desires, and ego.
- They rush you into oaths or vows.
- They're vague about who they are.
- They don't recognize you even if you've had prior interactions with them.

Because impostors are looking for "low-risk, high-rewards," they usually don't like getting caught.

WARDING

Warding is the act of creating a certain set of permissions and allowances for your space. To begin warding, first cleanse your space. This can be as simple as cleaning it with the intention of moving the energy, or using something like smoke cleansing or another method to get rid of any stagnant energy.

Wards need a minimum of three things: Instructions to follow; a battery to be powered by (such as a crystal charged in the sun); and a way to be attached to the space you're in (such as a wand or your finger). Speak your instructions out loud as you string your intention around the room with your finger or wand, starting with your battery and working your way back to it, like a circuit.

You can first write your instructions as a list if you'd like. Make sure to keep it as reference and so you can boost your wards later if they become stagnant. Be clear about what your wards should do, such as whether they should only allow certain entities to enter, and/or if they should kick out any entities for not obeying particular house rules (which you also specify). Make sure that only you can change the behavior and instructions of your wards.

CLOSING NOTES ON HEATHENRY

As you make your way into a veneration practice with Thor, consider these final words on the ongoing evolution of Norse polytheism...

Throughout this book, I mention "Heathenry" and "Norse Paganism." As of right now, these appear to be the most common descriptors to refer to neo-pagan practices and beliefs inspired by, or derived from, the folkloric customs, practices, and beliefs of the pre-Christian societies of the Nordic countries. What makes them different is subject to interpretation.

Currently, Heathenry is undergoing a period of rapid growth and development, with many people gravitating toward it. Perhaps the most common question I am asked by others is: "How do I become a Heathen?" I want to take a moment to address this question... or rather, to address the assumption that "being Heathen" is a matter of following instructions or conforming to a set of values or ideals.

Many people who come to this practice assume that Norse Paganism is done the same way we bake a cake—that a Heathen practice is a product of combining all the right ingredients. This is not the case. Rather, it is something more like a garden: It grows out of the space around us and the architecture of our lives.

Functionally speaking, this doesn't mean you have to follow certain instructions in order to be rewarded with an interpersonal relationship with Thor. Rather, your interpersonal relationship grows out of trying out different ways to venerate him and figuring out what's best for you

Regardless of what our path is and what we may call ourselves, the heart of spirituality is to find what works best for us by trying many different things.

GLOSSARY

In this book, I've chosen to use anglicized versions of the Old Norse names. Other books, however, may use the Old Norse. The glossary below gives both versions as well as a rough guide to pronunciation.

PRONUNCIATION OF OLD NORSE & ICELANDIC LETTERS

A, a	"Ah" as in "lava"
Á, á	"Ow" as in "owl" or "ouch" or "awl"
Æ, æ	"Aye" as in "eye" or "might"
Đ, ð	Voiced "th" as in "that" or "the"
É, é	"Yeh" as in "yet"
I, i	"Ih" as in "inn" or "bin"
Í, í	"Ee" as in "eel" or "eerie"
J, j	"Ye" as in "yard" or "your"
Ó, ó	"O" as in "oval" or "boat"
Ö, ö	"Uh" as in "enough"
Ǫ, ǫ	Same as ö
Œ, œ	Same as ö
Ú, ú	"Oo" as in "mood" or "rude" or "loot"
Ý, ý	Same as í
Þ, þ	Unvoiced "th" as in "thing" or "thaw"

A NOTE ABOUT "-R"

The "r" at the end of words such as "Jörmungandr" and "Óðr" are not fully pronounced. The trick is to start saying the letter and then "give up" halfway through.

GODS, GODDESSES, GIANTS, AND OTHER IMPORTANT FIGURES

English	Old Norse	
Aegir	Ægir	A giant who personifies the sea.
Alvis		A dwarf who claimed he was going to marry Thor's daughter, Thrud. Thor tricks him and he turns into stone.
Angrboda	Angrboða	Loki's consort, a giantess who gives birth to their three monstrous children: Fenrir, Hel, and Jormungand.
Aurvandil		The name of a giant whom Thor carried across the Elivagar rivers.
Authumbla	Auðumbla	The primordial cow that fed the giant Ymir.
Balder	Baldr	The shining god, said to be the fairest and best of all gods. Son of Odin.
Bestla		Odin's mother and Thor's grandmother, a giantess.

Bor	Borr	Odin's father and Thor's grandfather.
Brokk	Brokkr	A dwarf smith who worked the bellows when forging Mjolnir.
Buri	Búri	Odin's grandfather and Thor's great-grandfather, who was licked out of the ice by Authumbla.
Fenrir		The wolf who swallows Odin during Ragnarok.
Frey	Freyr	A warrior who traded his sword for his wife. He is associated with fertility, prosperity, masculinity, and kingship.
Freyja		A powerful and beautiful goddess. She is associated with love, beauty, magic, and war.
Frigg		The Allmother. She is associated with weaving, wisdom, and women's mysteries. Thor's stepmother.
Geirrod	Geirröðr	A giant-king who lives in Jötunheim. Thor and Loki visit his courts.
Gialp & Greip	Gjálp ok Greip	Daughters of the giant Geirrod, who were killed by Thor.
Grid	Gríðr	Vidarr's mother, a giantess. She lends Thor her belt of strength, her iron glove, and her staff before he confronts the giant Geirrod.
Groa	Gróa	A giantess who attempts to extract a whetstone stuck in Thor's head, only to be distracted by Thor's storytelling.
Heimdall	Heimdallr	The watchman of Asgard.
Hel		The goddess of death, who is half-maiden, half-corpse.
Hoenir	Hœnir	Odin's brother, who gives humanity the gift of sense. Also known as Vili.
Hrungnir		A giant with whom Thor battles. He fights Thor with a giant whetstone.
Hymir		A giant who owns a cauldron fetched by Thor.
Jarnsaxa	Járnsaxa	A giantess and Thor's consort.
Jord	Jörð	A giantess who personifies the Earth. Thor's mother.
Jormungand	Jörmungandr	The World Serpent, who encircles the Earth. Thor's archnemesis.
Logi		The personification of fire. He has an eating contest with Loki when Thor and Loki visit Utgard-Loki.
Loki		Asgard's resident mischief-maker. Thor's blood-uncle.
Modi & Magni	Móði ok Magni	Thor's children with Jarnsaxa, whose names mean "wrath" and "mighty." Together with their sister Thrud, they embody their father's characteristics.
Nott	Nótt	The personification of the night and Thor's grandmother.
Odin	Oðinn	The Allfather and Thor's father. He's the chief of the Aesir and associated with wisdom, war, poetry, madness, and death.

Roskva		Thor's servant. Sister to Thjalfi.
Sif		A goddess with long, golden hair. Thor's wife.
Sindri		The dwarf who makes Mjolnir, Draupnir, and Gullinbursti.
Skrymir	Skrýmir	A disguise of Utgard-Loki's. Thor and Loki slept in his mitten, thinking it was a cave.
Sons of Ivaldi		A set of dwarves skilled at smithing.
Surt	Surtr	The guardian of Muspelheim and greatest of the fire-giants.
Tanngrisnir & Tanngnjost	Tanngrisnir ok Tanngnjóstr	Thor's goats that pull his chariot.
Thjalfi	Þjálfi	Thor's servant and a swift runner.
Thor	Þórr	The thunder-god and protector of Midgard, who wields the hammer Mjolnir.
Thrud	Þrúðr	Thor's daughter with Sif, whose name means "strength."
Thrym	Þrymr	The giant who steals Thor's hammer.
Tyr	Týr	The one-handed god, who lost his hand to Fenrir. He and Thor went to fetch a cauldron.
Ullr		The hunter and bowman on skis. Thor's stepson.
Utgard-Loki	Útgarða-Loki	A giant illusionist who challenges Thor and Loki to different feats in his fortress, Utgard.

PLACES

English	Old Norse	
Alfheim	Álfheimr	The home of the light elves.
Asgard	Ásgarðr	The home of the Aesir.
Bifrost	Bifröst	The rainbow bridge that connects Asgard to Midgard.
Bilskirnir		The name of Thor's hall, said to have 540 rooms.
Elivagar rivers	Élivágar	The "poisonous" rivers that flow from Hvergelmir.
Helheim		The hall of the dead, where those who die of old age and sickness go.
Jötunheim	Jötunheimr	The home of the giants.
Midgard	Miðgarðr	["Middle Earth"] The home of people. The material world.
Muspelheim	Múspellsheimr	A fiery primordial world. Fire-giants live here.
Nidavellir	Niðavellir	The home of the dwarves.
Niflheim	Niflheimr	A cold and misty primordial realm of frost and ice.
Nordic countries, the		Norway, Sweden, Denmark, Iceland, Greenland, Finland, Åland, and the Faroe Islands.

Scandinavia		The historical name for a linguistic and cultural region in Northern Europe, mostly correlating with the Nordic countries, but also parts of Germany. Those from the Nordic countries still tend to refer to themselves as Scandinavian.
Sessrumnir	Sessrúmnir	One of Freyja's halls. It's also characterized as a field and a ship.
Thrudheim	Þrúðheimr	The country in which Thor's hall is located, meaning "world of strength."
Utgard	Utgarð	Hall of the giant Utgard-Loki.
Valhalla	Valhöll	The hall of the slain. Odin's hall, where fallen warriors go.
Vanaheim	Vanaheimr	Home of the Vanir.
Yggdrasil		The World Tree, which holds all realms.

THINGS, CONCEPTS, AND EVENTS

English	Old Norse	
Aesir	Æsir	The principal family of deities within the Norse pantheon.
Berserkers	Berserkir	["Bear-shirts"] Warriors who went into a wild, animalistic frenzy before battle.
Black elves	Svartálfar	Black elves, possibly a cognate with dwarves and dark elves. They are said to live underground and be blacker than pitch.
Brisingamen	Brísingamen	Freyja's beautiful necklace.
Dark elves	Dökkálfar	Elves who live underground and contrast with the Light Elves. See also *Black Elves*.
Draupnir		Odin's arm-ring, which drips eight gold rings just like it every ninth night.
Dwarves	Dvergr	Beings who live deep beneath the earth and are masters of craftwork.
Einherjar		The warriors of Valhalla.
Galdrastafir		Icelandic magical staves.
Giants	Jötnar	Beings who embody the wild, untamable landscapes and forces of the world.
Gleipnir		The fetters made of impossible things that bind Fenrir.
Heathenry		A neo-pagan spiritual movement centered on the beliefs, customs, and practices of various pre-Christian northern European societies.
	Járngreipr	["Iron grippers"] Thor's iron mitts.
Kenning		A kind of word play, which uses descriptive turns of phrase in place of a word, found in Old Norse poetry.
Land spirit	Landvættir	A spirit whose "body" is a certain area of land or land feature.

Light elves	Ljósálfar	Elves who are said to live in the realm of Alfheim and to be fairer than the sun to look at.
	Megingjörð	["Power-belt"] Thor's belt of strength.
Mjolnir	Mjölnir	["Crusher"] Thor's hammer, forged by the dwarves and the bane of giants.
Nisse		Friendly house spirits.
Norns, the	Nornir	Women who shape the course of fate and destiny.
Norse Paganism		A neo-pagan spirituality modeled after the beliefs, customs, and practices of the Norse people.
Offering	Blót	The act of making offerings to deities, ancestors, or spirits.
Ragnarok	Ragnarök	["The destiny of the gods"] The collapse of the Aesir's society.
Seid	Seiðr	A kind of Norse magic.
Thurs	Þurs	Giants who represent forces of nature that are actively hostile toward human life.
Tomte		See *Nisse.*
Trolls		A general word for a being who is "other." Can also be used to describe magic.
Valkyries	Valkyrjur	Women who ride over the battlefields and carry fallen warriors to Odin's hall, Valhalla, after they die.
Vanir		Another family of deities within the Norse pantheon, who fought a war with the Aesir in bygone times.
Viking Age, the		[793–1066 CE] A period marked by extensive sailing, trading, and raiding by the Norse people.
Wight	Vættr	A general term for "being" or "spirit."
Witch/Seeress	Völva (singular) Völur (plural)	["Staff-bearer"] A witch, seeress, or wise woman.

TEXTS

Our knowledge of the old Norse legends derives from a few main written sources, listed in bold type below. If you'd like to read them for yourself, I've specified which of the primary sources each "lay" or poem comes from.

Alvíssmál [1]	All-Wise's Sayings
Baldrs draumar [1] [3]	Balder's Dreams
Codex Regius, the	A manuscript from which the *Poetic Edda* is derived. It was written around 1270 CE.
Egils saga	Egil's saga. A medieval Icelandic saga. It's oldest manuscript dates back to 1250 CE.
Flateyjarbók	Book of Flatey. A medieval Icelandic manuscript compiled by two Christian priests in the 14th century.

Germania	[98 CE] A biased ethnography of the Germanic peoples written by the Roman historian and politician, Publius Cornelius Tacitus.
Gesta Danorum	The History of the Danes, written by Saxo Grammaticus in 1208 CE.
Gesta hammaburgensis ecclesiae pontificum	Deeds of the Bishops of Hamburg. By German medieval chronicler Adam of Bremen.
Grímnismál [1]	Grimnir's Sayings
Gróttasöngr [1]	The Mill's Song
Gylfaginning [2]	The Tricking of Gylfi
Hálfs saga ok hálfsrekka	The Saga of Halfr and His Heroes. A legendary saga about Halfr, who was one of Norway's most famous and legendary sea-kings.
Hárbarðsljóð [1]	The Lay of Harbard
Háttatal [2]	Tally of Meters
Hávamál [1]	Sayings of the High One
Heimskringla	A collection of sagas about Swedish and Norwegian kings of disputed authorship, though some scholars attribute it to Snorri Sturluson.
Hymiskviða [1]	The Lay of Hymir
Hyndluljóð [1]	The Lay of Hyndla
Lokasenna [1]	Loki's Quarrel
Lokka Þattur	Loki's Song. It is a Faroese ballad potentially dating back to the 14th century.
Njáls saga	Njal's saga. The longest and most highly developed of the sagas of the Icelanders.
Oddrúnargrátr [1]	Oddrun's lament. An Eddic poem, likely from the 11th century.
Poetic Edda, the	A compilation of anonymous Old Norse poetry, dating from before Scandinavia converted to Christianity.
Prose Edda, the	Also called the *Edda* or the *Elder Edda*. It was written by Snorri Sturluson around 1220 CE.
Rígsþula [1]	The Lay of Rig
Skáldskaparmál [2]	Poetic Diction, The Language of Poetry
Skírnismál [1]	The Lay of Skirnir
Sörla þáttr	The Tale of Sörlie, found in the *Flateyjarbók* manuscript.
Vafþrúðnismál [1]	The Lay of Vafthrudnir
Völundarkviða [1]	The Lay of Volund
Völuspá in skamma [1]	Short Prophecy of the Seeress
Völuspá [1]	The Prophecy of the Seeress
Ynglinga saga	A King's saga, written by Snorri Sturluson, about the royal Yngling dynasty, contained in the first section of *Heimskringla*.
Þrymskviða [1]	The Lay of Thrym

Key:

[1] - Found in the *Poetic Edda*

[2] - Found in the *Prose Edda*

[3] - Found in *Gesta Danorum*

INDEX

S

T

U

V

W

Y

AUTHOR'S ACKNOWLEDGMENTS

I'd like to thank my editor, Charlene Fernandes, for her support, patience, and grace during the writing of this book; as well as Elinor Ward for her excellent knowledge in Norse studies and for cross-checking manuscripts. I'd also like to thank Lily De Gatacre for facilitating this project to begin with, as well as Emma Harverson, Caroline West, Martina Calvio, Karin Skånberg, and Lorraine Dickey for bringing it to life. Lastly, I'd like to thank the Saxon Storyteller for all his fantastic illustrations; they have made me smile.

Thank you for reading and I hope you've enjoyed!

ABOUT THE ILLUSTRATOR

Matt Greenway is the illustrator of the Norse Gods series. He is known for his ability to capture the character of artifacts and historical figures and goes by "THE SAXON STORYTELLER" on the internet. His interests in Anglo Saxon, Celtic, and Norse mythologies and history have inspired his work for many years. He shares his passion for drawing mythology on Instagram @thesaxonstoryteller and illustrates content for the Nordic Mythology Podcast.